T0044565

Advance Praise for

FINE DREAMS

"In an age when domestic and personal dramas capture most literary attention, *Fine Dreams* breaks the mold, bravely and forthrightly investigating geo-religious and political history via the personal. Four kidnapped teenage schoolgirls guide us through the seemingly unbearable—appalling brutality and collective terror—toward life, death, and hope beyond. I read this book straight through. It was impossible not to."

—Robin McLean, author of *Pity the Beast*

"Masi writes with so much resolve, gravity, and unwavering sincerity that her debut novel, *Fine Dreams,* gave me almost constant chills."

—Catherine Lacey, author of *Biography of X*

"In *Fine Dreams,* Linda Masi's clear-eyed prose vividly renders the fates of five Nigerian schoolgirls caught up in violent clashes of religion and culture. A moving ghost story for our turbulent times, this powerful multi-voiced novel dives deep into the rapids of extremism, skillfully alternating between voices that each mount their separate bids for survival with whatever tools lie closest to hand. Affecting and intense, Masi's first novel may break readers' hearts wide open, but the resiliency of the human spirit that emanates from each page is sure to stitch them expertly, beautifully, back together."

—Katie Cortese, author of *Make Way for Her and Other Stories* and *Girl Power and Other Short-Short Stories*

FINE DREAMS

FINE DREAMS

LINDA N. MASI

UNIVERSITY OF MASSACHUSETTS PRESS
Amherst and Boston

Printed in the United States of America

ISBN 978-1-62534-792-3 (paper)

Designed by Sally Nichols
Set in Freight Text Pro
Printed and bound by Books International, Inc.

Cover design by adam b. bohannon

Library of Congress Cataloging-in-Publication Data

Names: Masi, Linda N., author.
Title: Fine dreams / Linda N. Masi.
Description: Amherst : University of Massachusetts Press, 2024. | Series: Juniper prize for fiction
Identifiers: LCCN 2023046504 (print) | LCCN 2023046505 (ebook) | ISBN 9781625347923 (paperback) | ISBN 9781685750671 (ebook) | ISBN 9781685750688 (ebook)
Subjects: LCSH: Teenage girls—Crimes against—Fiction. | Kidnapping victims—Fiction. | Nigeria—Fiction. | LCGFT: Novels.
Classification: LCC PR9387.9.M3755 F56 2024 (print) | LCC PR9387.9.M3755 (ebook) | DDC 823/.92—dc23/eng/20231023
LC record available at https://lccn.loc.gov/2023046504
LC ebook record available at https://lccn.loc.gov/2023046505

British Library Cataloguing-in-Publication Data
A catalog record for this book is available from the British Library.

Fine Dreams is a work of fiction. Unless otherwise indicated, all names, characters, businesses, places, events, and incidents in this book are either the product of the author's imagination or used in a fictitious manner. Any resemblance to actual events, incidents, or persons, living or dead, is entirely coincidental. Real acts of terrorism were captured as news pieces or as flashbacks. Acts of terrorism experienced by the novel's characters and the names of some of the towns and places are purely fictional.

For all who have been impacted by terrorism,
may light and peace grace your path.

CONTENTS

FINE DREAMS

PROLOGUE: 2014

It was Monday. I had spent the weekend at home, my bad habit, and was glad to be back at the boarding house at St. Thomas Memorial School in Kasar Lafiya. The bell for midday class break gonged. When Auntie Maryam, our history teacher, exited the class, I dug into the side pocket of my school bag and pulled out the clipping I had cut from one of the newspapers Mother had brought home the Friday before. It told the story of two girls in the neighboring town of Chibok who had escaped from their terrorist abductors' camp a month before. The girls lamented to the journalist that the terrorists, who were training their prisoners as sharpshooters, had forced the stronger girls at the camp to use the weaker girls for target practice. So many questions about the situation filled my mind, and I was dying to ask my friends Aquamarine, Gaddo, and Grace about their thoughts.

Still, when they asked if I would come with them to the tuck shop to buy snacks, I shook my head and remained at my desk, clipping in hand. The story was raw in my mind; every time I reread it, the hair on my arms rose, and I shivered as if creepy-crawlies were inching over me. For some reason, the story reminded me of what we'd just been learning from Auntie Maryam: how Hades, Greek god of the underworld, had kidnapped Persephone, goddess of spring, and made her his queen.

Grace's eyes lingered on the paper in my hand. In her brash voice, she said, "Tell us the news already, Kubra." I wanted to tell them about the kidnapped girls, but instead I chuckled and asked, "If you were Persephone, kidnapped by Hades, what would you do?" The girls burst into laughter, shook their heads, and trooped out of the classroom, promising to bring back Fanta and *kuli-kuli* to cool my brain from too much schoolwork. Usually, my random questions triggered hearty arguments, but this time they were in a hurry to get to the tuck shop, which was always packed with students during the thirty-minute break. It could be hard to buy food for lunch before the break ended.

I crumpled the clipping and shoved it back into my school bag. I guess my question did sound silly. Even though the story of Persephone and Hades was only a fable, I couldn't help but see it reflected in the tale of those girls from Chibok. Like Persephone, were they always under watch by their captors? How could she have freed herself from Hades? Intelligence was definitely one necessary skill. Was deviousness another? I was eager to hear what ideas my friends would come up with. I also hoped the Fanta they would bring me would be very cold. The May heat in Kasar Lafiya was unforgiving.

PART ONE:
2015

KUBRA'S ERRAND

At 11 p.m. on January 8, a couple of months after my death, I sat beside Mother on my bare mattress and watched her murmur my name as she squeezed my old blue-and-white checkered school uniform to her bosom. She pressed the cotton pinafore to her face, muffling her weeping, while Danladi, my little brother, slept soundly in the opposite bed. In her lap sat the glass jar containing my cremated ashes. They looked like gritty gray sand, and I wished that they, along with the memory of that fateful night, were hidden underground somewhere, away from my view. Sometimes I wondered what would happen if Mother were to bury my ashes instead of saving them in the jar. Would a proper burial in a grave end my endless hovering on earth? But at other times I was glad she had made the jar a monument of her love for me. Even though her weeping always pricked my heart, I selfishly liked knowing that she wept over me. I felt treasured. But I also understood that her constant tears were wearing out her body and her mind, and this made me feel that my ghost had overstayed its presence on earth. I hoped to find a way to rest, to discover a place that wasn't this limbo in which I and so many other ghosts were trapped. Now I wrapped an arm around Mother's rocking shoulders. With my other hand I patted her grizzled hair, arranged in its loose *hannu-biyu* rows, and I whispered that my death was not her fault. But of course, she couldn't hear me. She couldn't see me. She couldn't feel my touch.

Hour after hour, Mother sat in this same spot, weeping. But when a neighbor's rooster began to crow its sunrise song, she sighed, stood up, and carried my uniform and the jar out of the room. I didn't need to follow her to know that she would return the jar to the glass-faced cupboard in the sitting room where she had arrayed our family portraits, my sprint trophies and medals, photographs of Aquamarine, Grace, Gaddo, and me holding our trophies. She would return the uniform to my suitcase in the box room, where it stood beside Father's trunk, and then go to the kitchen to boil a kettle of water on the kerosene stove for Danladi's morning bath. It was her nightly routine to whisper my name into my uniform and weep. Perhaps it was an effort to plaster together her broken heart. But I wished she would sleep more before she went to work at St. Thomas, my old school for aspiring teachers and educators, where she was the administrative vice principal. Big black circles, like deflated inner tubes, had entrenched themselves around her eyes, and her cheeks were hollowed out as though some monster were eating her flesh from the inside out.

Danladi, still peacefully asleep, rubbed the edge of his jaw with his wrist for a moment, most likely to soothe the sting of a mosquito bite. I looked away from him to the black strip at the corner of the glass window where the flowered curtain failed to shut out the dark sky. The sky reminded me of the darkness that had engulfed me on that fateful day in early October 2014. I don't know who fired the rocket-propelled grenade that killed me—whether it was someone from the military or one of the weasels who abducted women and young girls and lived in shacks and tin bunkers in the Sahelian forests.

On the Friday evening of my death, Major Danjuma, Mother's admirer, had telephoned to say that he wouldn't be able to visit as usual and bring us the packet of *suya* he liked to share with us. The police force, he said, was embarking on an intense three-day patrol in the town, but he promised to visit the following week. At the time I was attaching the toy tires I'd cut from my old flip flops onto a cardboard army truck I had made for Danladi. Our neighbor, Mama Lakhmi, who lived three houses away, was visiting Mother, and Mother was inviting her to eat something. Mama Lakhmi turned down the offer, Mother insisted, and finally her visitor agreed to drink a Sprite. Mother said to me, "Kubra, take this money and go to Malam Balarabe's kiosk and buy Sprite for Mama Lakhmi. And don't be long."

"I want Fanta," said Danladi. He was six years old and had just started primary 1 that term. I wanted a Fanta, too, but I didn't mention this because I hoped to drink out of Danladi's when I poured it into a cup for him. In the past, Mother had disciplined me for seizing the chance to ask for my own refreshments when we entertained guests in our home. "It shows poor child training, and makes you a long throat," she would drone. Well, I thought she needed to give Danladi some better child training now because I remembered receiving my first warnings at his age.

But Mother did not admonish him. She just gave me two 50-naira notes to buy a bottle of Fanta and another of Sprite.

As I left the sitting room, Danladi was excitedly pulling his new toy truck by its short leash, the black shoelace from my old sneakers, into the corner of the sitting room by the window. "Po-po-po-po-poo, army-army. *Clerout. Clerout*," he ordered, bossing around some invisible street urchins and stragglers as he played his favorite game.

Meanwhile, Mother and Mama Lakhmi were arguing about the number of people who had died in a car bombing in Babban-Gari several months ago. Terrorists had driven a Volkswagen Golf loaded with explosives toward five buses packed with Christians who were traveling to the southeast region of the country. After striking one of the buses, the car had exploded, and the inferno had spread to others, which were still filled with passengers. Mama Lakhmi said she'd heard that twenty-five had been killed, but reporters for the BBC in Hausa had said twenty-two. According to Mother, the *Guard,* our local newspaper, claimed that sixty people had been killed. My take was that, whether twenty-two, twenty-five, or sixty, people had died without reason.

I shut the door and headed out for the sodas.

The sun had sunk below the stretch of rusted aluminum roofs that surrounded our house, but a deep orange halo remained in the darkening blue sky. The air smelled of petrol: everywhere, there were dark patches of fresh fuel on the asphalt and the red clay verge. The fumes made my eyes water as I strode across the road to Malam Balarabe's kiosk. Even the dirty water that trickled in the street's open gutters was filmy with petrol. Perhaps a vehicle with a fuel leak had driven by, one like the rickety taxi whose rusty pinhole leaks had messed up the street a couple of months earlier. But something strange was going on. Near an armored tank, recaptured by the military from the weasels, several armed soldiers were searching a house, questioning residents about their links to the weasels. Another group of soldiers was stationed at the opposite end of the street. Only a few passersby were outside, which was quite unusual.

Malam Balarabe's little kiosk was perched on the left side of the Habu Hassan mosque. It was open, but I didn't see the usual moonlike curve of the malam's white crocheted kufi at the window, and he hadn't yet turned on the light. A few men were already inside the mosque, seated on their prayer mats. Perhaps he was busy in the backyard, I thought. I resolved to wait until 6 p.m., about twenty minutes, in case he showed up to lock his shop before heading to prayers.

I saw three men seated inside a dark red Nissan parked close to the kiosk. Two had huge beards and the third wore a full face mask that covered his entire head. I thought they, too, were waiting to buy something from Malam Balarabe's kiosk. But then they jumped out of their car. With the driver holding a long duffle bag slung across his shoulder, the three hastened across the street and knocked on the door of our house! I had never seen any of them before. And I didn't like the way they walked into our house like kings when the door opened.

I thought it wouldn't hurt to snoop around the men's vehicle, peek through the windows. They might pose like princes, but the inside of their car could be a messy, stinky waste dump like Mr. Zubairu's. He was the agriculture teacher at our school, and he claimed to be some kind of prince in his village. Once he gave Aquamarine and me a ride to town during the first term of ninth grade. His car had a funky smell, and fat brown cockroaches crept all over the seats, our legs, our clothes, even the roof.

When I looked into the men's car, the first thing I saw was a stuffed dachshund lying on its side in the driver's seat. I smiled, thinking Danladi would like it until I spotted the muzzle of a handgun peeping from its rear end. I staggered backward. My heart seemed to jump from my chest and hit the ground. Mother? Danladi? Who are these men? What do they want with us? I wanted to yell so that Mother—everyone—would hear my warning, but I felt as if I were gagged. I looked again at the car and saw several large nylon tote bags in the back seat. Nails poked out from the sides of the bags. I also saw that the vehicle's boot was not completely shut. The hatch rested on top of five odd-looking cylinders, some cases of dynamite, and four plastic jerrycans that smelled of petrol.

I thought, run and alert the soldiers! I took two steps away from the car and then a grenade struck the boot. Instantly, explosions—the car, the cylinders, the jerrycans of fuel, dynamite, the nails, me. The petrol stains in the street became balls and streams of fire. Car, kiosk, mosque, a few houses ignited, and people ran for safety.

The explosion wrenched my spirit out of my body and, with nowhere to rest, it hovered over the eruption, searching for my body, trying to enter back in. But my left thigh was in the gutter down the street, being eaten by yellow-red fire. My flip-flopped feet remained intact at the spot where I'd met the blast. A slab of my torso was plastered onto a beam dangling from the gaping roof of the house opposite the mosque. My right hand was consumed by a fresh string of explosions that now went off in the house beside the mosque. My head and part of my left shoulder lay a distance away in the center of the road, a mass of fire, burning, burning, burning. A few half-burnt brightly colored candy wrappers and biscuit packets, sweets that had once filled the plastic jars in Malam Balarabe's kiosk, lay about my burning head.

What came to my mind was to run to our house and alert Mother, but instead I found myself clumsily floating toward the house at alarming speed. My feet, my hands, every part of my body, though they seemed whole, were opaque and, in some places, faded to transparency. Yet my actual body parts were burning all over the street! *Hauka ne!* Crazy! I saw that the blast had broken all of our windows, so I glided through one and saw one of the men with the huge beards pointing a rifle at Mother's head as she knelt in our sitting room with her arms raised in surrender. The second bearded man pointed a rifle at Mama Lakhmi, who was kneeling and quaking. A duffle bag lay unzipped and empty in the corner.

"My daughter is outside!" Mother cried. "There's been an explosion!"

"Shut up, woman!" the man said and poked her forehead with the muzzle of his rifle. "You only speak when and if I permit you to. And you are going nowhere until I say so."

I yelled, waved my hands in the air, but no one seemed to notice me, not even Mother. I tried to snatch the rifle, but my fingers swished through it as if the rifle did not exist. I stared at my empty hands and moaned. I commanded my solid flesh to fill up the translucent spaces, but nothing happened. I understood now that my solid flesh would forever remain lost to me. The moment felt as black as night. No. This is a dream, I thought. I retreated into the corner and knocked my head against the wall, as I used to do when I was younger and Mother had scolded me for some wrongdoing. I would use my pain to get her attention, and it usually worked: she would run to me, speak gently, give me a hug me. I hoped to feel that intense pain again, to catch Mother's attention again. But my head slid through the wall, and I felt nothing. Absolutely nothing. Mother didn't look in my direction. Her eyes were wild and red and fixed on the man's dusty black boots.

The man pulled back the rifle and said, "This is only a warning visit, Mrs. Sadau Fatai-Ehis. There will be no second warning. We will strike suddenly if you do not do as we say. You must either step down from your position as vice principal of St. Thomas Memorial School or stay in the position and stop making trouble."

Breathing heavily, Mother stared at the man. "Why don't you go to the Ministry of Education and tell them to sack me?"

"*Toh*," said the man. "You are commanding us, eh?"

She shook her head and lowered her gaze to the man's feet. She blinked rapidly but no tears fell. Her chest rose and fell rapidly.

"Your problem is that you talk too much. You don't know how to stay out of matters that do not concern you."

Mother looked up and said shakily, "The school's board of administration threatened to fire teachers from the south just because they are southerners and follow a different religion. Are we not one Nigeria?"

Instantly, the man burst into a string of obscenities. But the other man in the room interrupted him, warning that they were running out of time and that the police would soon be arriving to investigate the explosion.

Where was the third man who had walked into the house? And where was Danladi? Danladi's truck lay overturned on the floor by the window. I went toward our bedroom to search for him. The door was shut, but I floated through it. *Hauka ne!* Crazy! There was the man, seated on my bed with Danladi beside him. He had pulled off his mask. There was a nasty scar across his left cheek that resembled a centipede, and his beard was scraggly.

"Your mother did something bad," the man said to Danladi. "We do not want to hurt her or you. We only want to tell her to change her ways."

Terrified, Danladi stared at the man's scar.

"When your mother catches you doing something bad, she tells you to stop it. Sometimes with a loud voice, doesn't she?"

Danladi nodded.

"That is why we are here," said the man.

Suddenly there was a loud bang on the front door, and I rushed back into the sitting room. Three soldiers and two policemen stormed in and immediately arrested the two men there.

"Another with a mask is in the room with my son," Mother said, but when the police surged into the bedroom, only Danladi was seated on the bed. They asked him about the man, and he pointed to the open window.

Back in the sitting room, the officers told Mother and Mama Lakhmi that someone had died in the explosion and asked if they were missing a family member.

"Kubra!" Mother cried. Her eyes bulged. She grabbed Danladi's hand and shoved him toward Mama Lakhmi, then ran outside.

Onlookers crowded the street, choking and coughing amid billows of black smoke and gasoline fumes. Night had closed in. The sky was moonless and starless, but the street was filled with light as people waved lamps and cell phones. Three Hilux police trucks were lit up by the officers' headlamps. Everywhere, policemen and soldiers worked to keep the crowd from tramping over the crime scene, and people were pointing out various objects, wondering if Mother would identify them as belonging to her missing daughter.

When Mother saw the scattered scraps of my blue and pink dress, she ran crazily into the crowd. "Kubra? Kubra?" she called, until someone pointed at a smoking, glowing ember that still held the oblong form of a human head. Mother knelt and touched it, burning her hands. She flicked away the pain, then patted at the scorched bones and flesh along the jaw, finding, among the charred teeth, a familiar broken incisor. Now she knew.

Shrieking at the skies, calling my name, Mother slumped to the ground, packed ashes and sand around my head, and poured ashes and sand on her own head, on her own body. I was there, kneeling beside her, but she couldn't see me. I threw my arms around her, touched her hands, her face, tried to wipe away her tears, but she did not feel my touch.

For days after my death, Mother was unable to sleep. She would jump suddenly from her bed at odd hours of the night, grab a flashlight, go outside, hoping to find me hiding from her in the darkness. But she was usually held back by the policemen who had been ordered to patrol our street and keep a close watch on our house. Eventually, when Mama Lakhmi arrived to keep vigil for a couple of days, Mother stopped trying to find me.

Two weeks after my death, the man with the centipede scar still remained at large. Meanwhile, the police had identified the vehicle loaded with explosives as stolen and as evidence of ties with terrorist groups. But they had been unable to identify the two men with huge beards they had arrested to the vehicle. The men had vehemently denied having anything to do with the vehicle or the explosive materials in the car. *Liars!* They had simply been charged with unlawful possession of weapons and criminal intimidation and were locked up in the maximum security prison at Birnin Haske. Then local residents offered more information. Some said that certain weasels had meant to fire the grenade at the armored tank up the street but had missed their target and hit the car instead. Others said that soldiers, who suspected that certain locals were supporting the weasels, had themselves been responsible for firing the grenade. The military denied the allegations and promised to investigate.

When Major Danjuma heard the news of my death, he was angry with himself. He felt he had disappointed Mother, crushed her soul. The police patrol that had been organized to rid Kasar Lafiya of terrorists had inadvertently led to my death, yet there was no one to hold accountable. He visited during the first week of December, his eyes sunken and red. He sat beside Mother on the couch in the sitting room, saying little and patting her hand soothingly whenever she started talking to herself about how my death still felt like a dream. Just before he left, he told her, "I am very sorry for your loss. It is my loss too. Kubra was such a gem." Then he walked out to his car, shoulders drooping. Though he didn't return for weeks, he had an errand boy deliver provisions to her and Danladi every other week.

On December 23, the military released its final report, stating that there was insufficient evidence and they would not pursue the case. Mother saw this as a failure of justice, but she also blamed herself for sending me on the errand. She no longer offered refreshments to visitors, even on Christmas Day. She hated the sight of soft drinks and no longer allowed Danladi to drink them, restricting him to mangoes, dates, oranges, and other fruits in season. Yet even months after my death, he kept asking her, "Mami, when will Kubra come back with the Fanta?"

He finally stopped when she showed him the glass jar with my ashes, and my teeth in an envelope. In a grave voice she had said, "This is what the big fire left us of Kubra."

Days after New Year's Day, weasels in the region became bolder in their attacks, thanks to clumsy counterattacks by the military. The governor announced that all schools in our state would shut down starting on March 2. The town of Kasar Lafiya would be placed under curfew to curb the weasels' rampant abductions.

Mother and Danladi had a quick breakfast of oats at six o'clock on the morning of January 9. Then Mother dropped Danladi off at his school and headed for St. Thomas Memorial School, where she continued to serve as the vice principal. She apologized for being five minutes late to this first staff meeting of the term. The meeting hadn't gone on for long when the principal and a few other officials announced that the girls in my class who were preparing to write their general certificate practicum exams in May and June would continue with their planned extension classes, thus flouting the governor's orders. Mother opposed this, citing the danger to the girls. She reminded her colleagues that more than two hundred and fifty schoolgirls from Chibok had been kidnapped the year before, an incident that had drawn international indignation and birthed the #BringBackOurGirls Movement. She warned that they should take wiser steps for utmost safety. I agreed.

Before my death, I'd planned to become a history teacher like Auntie Maryam or a school administrator like Mother. Her passion for her job had been my biggest inspiration. Yet the day after the staff meeting, Mother received a note from the administrative secretary charging her with neglect of duty. She was asked to respond to the accusation within twenty-four hours. Clearly, this was a setup. *Rube!* That was what I called the administration's stinky antics.

The incident in question had happened during the previous term. Danladi had developed a hacking cough, and Mother had taken him to a doctor, fearing that he had pneumonia. The doctor's series of tests had consumed most of the day, so she had been unable to return to work. Now she showed the secretary the doctor's report as well as a photocopy of the signed hospital logbook. In response, the secretary said that the query committee would get back to Mother after concluding their investigations. Until then, she would be on indefinite paid leave, starting on February 1.

A few days later, Mother traveled to the Ministry of Education in Birnin Haske, the state capital, to report the matter. Officials there promised to deal with her case as soon as possible. However, nothing happened, and January came to an end.

February arrived, and Mother waited at home for the ministry's response. Meanwhile, the school was preparing for the inter-house sports competition, scheduled for the last Saturday of the month. During practice on February 4, I hung around to see who would be chosen as my replacement on the 400-meter senior relay team.

In seventh grade, when Aquamarine, Grace, Gaddo, and I had arrived at the school, we had been selected by our Red House boarding master, Mr. Okorie, to form the 400-meter junior team. Since then we had been inseparable friends and teammates. For months after my death, my friends had refused to set foot on the field. They told Mr. Okorie to find another team, said that they couldn't stand the sight of the track without me. But when Mother learned of the trouble this was causing, she visited the girls in their dormitory and told them that, by not running, they were setting fire to one of my dreams: to win the golden cup for Red House for the sixth time. Mother's words lightened their hearts and lessened their guilt.

After eight different girls competed in the selection race, Mr. Okorie chose Safiya, a new girl from Ilorin, as my replacement. Her family had moved to Kasar Lafiya two years ago and now worked in the fishing business. In her speed trials, she matched my second-best performance, completing the sprint in 1 minute, 8 seconds, beating Gaddo's best time of 1 minute, 12 seconds. But she fell far behind Grace's 60-second best and Aquamarine's 55-second achievement.

Safiya and Gaddo were seventeen, one year older than Aquamarine, and me, while Grace at fifteen, was inches taller than everyone else on the team. Over the years, Gaddo had sometimes shone on the track, but on other days her mood swings had damaged her performance. My own mood swings had mostly occurred when I thought of my father's desertion. Outraged all over again, I would run as if I were stomping on his head and, surprisingly, achieved my all-time best record in one of those moments. Grace, in contrast, ran like a horse, and Aquamarine was simply the queen of the track—light as powder with legs like motorcycles. Competitors used to get fooled by her short stature, thinking that their own long legs would easily beat her. But before they knew it, she was a cloud of dust ahead of them.

On the Saturday of the inter-house competition, Safiya broke my all-time best with a 1 minute, 2 second finish. I was happy for her and for the team, though also jealous. It's not easy to admit that one's replacement is better, but I owned up to it. Safiya was good. Grace and Aquamarine were on fire. Even though poor Gaddo was likely caught up in one of her mood swings, her 1 minute, 13 second finish didn't stop the team from clinching the golden cup, our team's sixth. The other Red House girls began to chant our song:

Dynamic four, unbeatable,
Red House, Winning House.

My friends then chanted along, hopping and dancing in a circle, holding up the golden cup together. On their left wrists they wore red rubber bangles with little white heart-shaped paper cutouts inscribed with *"RIP Kubra"* in glossy pink ink. My friends, they had remembered. Pink was my favorite color. Then Safiya stopped and said, "Let's add Kubra to the song. I'm not sure I would have had this spot if she were still with us." The other girls nodded, and Grace hollered the new line to the other Red House girls, who took the cue:

Dynamic five, unbeatable,
Red House, Winning House.

Mr. Okorie stood clapping for the girls, smiling as the Red House students ran around the field and then ran to their dormitory in celebration. I smiled too. Safiya became my friend that day. Of course, she didn't know this.

March 10 marked the five-month anniversary of my death. I still worried about why I had not found the key to my resting place, and I hoped that, by visiting the scene of my accident, exactly five months later, I might find some clues, I hovered over the street and discovered that much had changed. It was rowdier, and there was a stronger military presence. Where the abandoned armored tank had once sat, two policemen had now set up a checkpoint, stopping vehicles to search their boots and scan their luggage. But they also intervened in other situations. As I watched, a man on a motorcycle knocked down a woman at the corner, but instead of helping her up and apologizing, he threatened her. Quickly the police discovered that he had three AK-47 rifles tucked underneath the padding of the motorcycle seat. They called for backup and sent the man to the station.

Malam Balarabe had rebuilt his kiosk, and now he sat inside listening to Arabic and Indian music. I hovered closer and admired the shiny wrappings on the new candies he now sold. I had never tasted some of them. The mosque, too, was up and running again, and some of the damaged houses had all been rebuilt. But the crater in the road, created by the explosion, had not been patched up. It was even a few inches wider and filled with red muddy water.

Three almajiri children stopped close to the kiosk, holding out their begging bowls to receive 50-naira notes from a young man who was passing by. As the children trudged on, the man crossed the road and hastened into Mama Lakhmi's house. I noticed that his hair was bushy, his beard scraggly, and there was a dark mark on his left cheek. Moments later, Mama Lakhmi and the man walked out of her house together, and then I saw the man's face clearly. The mark on his cheek resembled a centipede. He spoke to Mama Lakhmi, promising to see her later that evening, and then walked away. When Mama Lakhmi went into our house to visit Mother, I followed her.

After exchanging pleasantries, Mama Lakhmi handed Mother a small bottle of a highly concentrated germicide, a disinfectant she had made herself. She had started her own chemical-supplies business the year before, after resigning from her job as a lab attendant at my school. Mother thanked her, gave her some naira notes, and put the bottle away. Then Mama Lakhmi asked Mother about her plans, for the school had refused to call her back to work and she had yet to hear from the Ministry of Education. Mother replied that she planned to go back to Birnin Haske, ask to see the governor in person, and plead for his intervention.

"When do you plan to leave?" asked Mama Lakhmi.

"I don't know yet," Mother said. "Why?"

"Oh," said the neighbor, flustered. "Just—."

"I am more concerned that they are putting the lives of all those girls in danger. I wish I could do something about it," said Mother.

"Let us hope nothing bad happens," said Mama Lakhmi.

"That is my greatest wish, *gaba ɗaya*—completely!" Mother agreed. She was setting up a small blackboard at the corner of the sitting room, and now she called Danladi to come sit for his lesson.

I sat there listening to them talk, as I had on the night of my death, until Mama Lakhmi got up to leave. Then I followed her to her house, where the young man sat waiting for her in her small sitting room crowded with furniture and whatnots.

"She plans to meet the governor in person soon, but she didn't say when she would make the trip," said Mama Lakhmi.

The man scratched his beard and said, "You have to press her so we know when to ambush her vehicle." He sneered. "That hopeless woman who married a kafir from the south only for him to abandon her and her children: we will teach her a good lesson on keeping the Holy Faith when we send her to one of the camps."

"She is worried about the safety of the girls," said Mama Lakhmi.

The man smirked and got up to leave.

"Farouk," said Mama Lakhmi. "None of the girls will be killed?"

"They will be sent where they are meant to be," he said without expression. "With their new husbands instead of that stupid school."

After he left, Mama Lakhmi sat silently and chewed her lower lip.

Traitor! I screeched at Mama Lakhmi. *Stay away from my mother! Stay away from my brother! Stay away from my friends!* But, of course, she didn't hear me. She got up, walked into her kitchen, loaded her plate with mounds of jollof rice, and began to munch like a donkey.

I rushed outside, but Farouk had sped away on a motorcycle.

Someone needed to stop this evil plan. What would happen to my classmates, my friends—Aquamarine, Grace, Gaddo, Safiya? Mother couldn't see or hear me. Who would save them? What would their future be?

AQUAMARINE

Aquamarine rubbed her eyes with the back of her hand to reassure herself that she was not dreaming and read the letter in her other hand for the fifth time. It was the fourth Saturday in the month of March, and she was among the grade 12 girls who were prepping for their general certificate practicum exams in the dormitories. She had received the letter at about noon the day before, when Mr. Titus, the school's postmaster, had delivered mail for the girls at the mai guardi's hut. The bold, elegant, right-slanting handwriting was her mother's, and the letter was signed *your loving mother, Dorathy Adannaya Ahia.*

After ten years of separation and silence, Aquamarine felt as if she were seated before her mother, holding her hand instead of this crisp white lined paper. Locking eyes with her words was material evidence that her mother was alive. Yet Aquamarine had written to her mother in mid-January; why had it taken two months for her mother to send this reply? And then to receive this response—*Don't visit me at Enugu. Remain with your auntie in Kasar Lafiya*—after all the years apart! Aquamarine held her breath for a moment, trying to ease the knot in her chest, then exhaled slowly. She remembered that she had slept last night with the letter spread on her chest, stupidly hoping for a miraculous change in its message, humming "Veni, Veni, Emmanuel" to herself until she fell asleep.

She folded the letter, stuffed it into the envelope, and shoved it into the mesh bag in her suitcase. Best to forget these words, this anxiety, until her exams were over in mid-June. Maybe the next time she unfolded the letter, the word *don't* would have moved from the beginning of the first sentence to the beginning of the second.

Aquamarine worked to close the zipper on the mesh bag, squeezing its bulky sides to ease the task. The bag contained numerous papers she considered private or special. There was a draft copy of the letter she had posted to her mother, expressing her deep desire to reunite with her in Enugu after exams were over. There were test papers and tuition receipts. At the bottom of the bag there was a worn 50-naira note folded into a neat square. A piece of white paper peeked through a tear in the bill, but Aquamarine could not remember what it was or why she had folded it inside the note. She reopened the bag, fished out the money, and read the paper:

3 medium mudus of rice—N1,500
1 large mudu of garri—N500
fresh red pepper (1 small mudu)—N100
grinding of pepper—N30
~~yams (2 tubers)—N900~~
salt (1 sachet)—N50

She sighed. It was a list of items that Auntie Ijeoma had sent her to purchase at the Gwagwalala market just before the term had begun in January. As usual, her auntie had refused to give her any transport fare. "Children nowadays are lazy. When I was your age, we used to save money for our parents by choosing to trek three miles to school and three miles back," Auntie Ijeoma had said, daintily opening the door for her.

Aquamarine's hike to the market had taken more than an hour, on roads with little police presence. Usually, at the Muari post, the last junction before the path that led to the market, she would see a stout policeman with dusky black skin and three long lines etched into each of his cheeks, tribal scars that belied his jovial personality. She didn't know his name and usually saluted him simply as "Sergeant," while he would hail her as "Yellow Pawpaw" because of her light ocher skin. At other times, he would shout, "My color, you come market?" which usually made her laugh. Then he would say, "Fine girl like you should always have a smile on her face," and she would nod and go on her way.

But on that day another policeman stood in Sergeant's position. This new one was questioning a taxi driver on the other side of the road when she passed by. By the time she reached the market her lower lip was split down the middle, courtesy of the cold, dry hamarttan winds. Her legs ached, and her sandals were dusty and red. But the steam of anger at her auntie lessened after she sighted a small group of almajiri children eating rotten bananas and moldy bread on the streetcorner, their begging bowls on the ground beside them. She walked into the market and, in a bargaining match with a rice seller, beat down the price of rice to 1,400 naira. As she retraced her steps toward home, she gave the almajiri children 50 naira and felt no guilt about keeping the remaining balance of 50 naira for herself.

Now, as she looked at the paper, Aquamarine brushed her thumb over the line canceling out *yams*. She racked her brain over why Auntie Ijeoma had crossed them out but could not remember. She looked at the word itself, the tail of the *y* forming a big loop that curved back up like a teardrop earring. The only thing she admired about Auntie Ijeoma was her handwriting, the beautiful loops on *j* and *g*, her *a* as smooth as a periwinkle shell. During the summer she had turned thirteen Aquamarine had used some of Auntie Ijeoma's longer lists as models for improving her own handwriting, which resembled chicken scratches in dirt. But she'd never quite reached the mark.

Aquamarine crumpled up the paper, but then a thought struck her and she smoothed out the list again and studied the writing. Dipping into her mesh bag, she retrieved the letter from her mother. With the letter in one hand and the list in the other, she examined the words. The handwriting was identical.

Jeering from outside cut through her thoughts. Kneeling on her bed, she peered through the netting over the window beside her bunk. All of the girls from the dormitories seemed to be clustered around the mai guardi's post beside the gates. Aquamarine looked at Grace's messy, empty bed next to hers. Gaddo's bed across from Grace's was also empty; so was Safiya's tidy bed, in Kubra's former space. All of the other beds in the room were empty too. Aquamarine wondered how she had failed to notice that the girls had left. She refolded the letter and the list, tucked them into the mesh bag and back in her suitcase, and hurried out to join the group.

Aquamarine, who served as deputy head girl, made her way to the front of the crowd until she was standing beside Asmau, the head girl. The crowd was spellbound, with some of the girls leaning against the large rectangular water tank beside the gate to get a better view. At the door of his hut the mai guardi, a tiny man, was telling a story, claiming that he had seen more than thirty old women selling bloody red meat to many students in the dead of last night. According to him, none of the students who had gone to that market had returned. However, the girls had already identified two big holes in his tale. He claimed that the buying and selling had happened on the giant baobab tree behind the dormitories, which was clearly impossible. Moreover, no students were missing.

"It must have been a dream, Mai Guardi," Asmau tried to persuade him.

"*Haba*, Asmau," he replied. "Me, I know the difference of dream from trance." He tugged at the bags under his eyes with his fingers. "My eyes no see sleep from night till morning."

"Of course, Mai Guardi." Asmau nodded, thin-lipped.

Aquamarine shook her head. Several times in the past year, Asmau had been tempted to report the mai guardi's drunkenness to the school authorities. Everyone knew he was only a ceremonial guard. The armed policemen who watched the main gates did the real job.

The mai guardi, rubbing at the bags under his eyes, turned his head toward Aquamarine. His eyes were like red glass beads. The sour smell of *burukutu* lingered on his breath, and an odor of urine clung to his clothes.

Gaddo cocked her head at an unlabeled brown bottle underneath the mai guardi's wooden bench, his bed during his night watch, and gave a wry smile. Aquamarine brushed a hand over her short afro and watched a laden mosquito straggle out of the shade beneath the bench into the soft sunlight lighting up Gaddo's cornrows. Its translucent abdomen was red and engorged.

Then Gaddo leaned forward, snatched the empty bottle, and waved it in the mai guardi's face. "This bottle must have been filled with something *delicious* last night."

The mai guardi scratched at the chalky hair on his balding head and dropped his eyes. A pained look crossed his face as he spat curses at the bottle—*Mugunta! Jarabawa! Shege!*

Aquamarine fought back a giggle, but Safiya and the other girls did not hide their smiles.

"Me, I drink only small, *kadan*," the mai guardi mumbled and looked up again. His eyes bulged. "*Wallahi*, the girls, no one returned from the market."

"But how did the women and girls climb the tree?" a girl named Jemimah asked. She often sneaked out to night parties in town, after having bribed the mai guardi with *burukutu*.

"They just disappeared and reappeared," he said, waving his hands.

Everyone burst into laughter.

"*Ehen*, Kasar Lafiya witches have taken to the skies," said Jemimah.

"This is a spiritual battle," said Safiya with a serious look. "We have to pray."

"Number 1 prayer point," chimed in Ntala. "I want to pass my exams with all *A*s in June." Ntala had pale albino skin, hazel eyes, and long black hair and was from Rivers State, in the southern region of the country. Grace had nicknamed her "Mami-water" after her state of origin, a corruption of Mami Wata, the African water deity.

"Mami-water," said Grace, "your first prayer point should be to conquer the spirit of dozing that possesses you whenever you open any of your textbooks."

"*Shegiya*." Ntala flashed a flared palm at Grace.

Laughter rose but soon died down, when Grace hollered in a panicky voice, "Safiya is missing."

For a moment, silence towered. Each girl looked carefully to the left and to the right, fearing that this was true.

"Yaah," Safiya said, appearing from behind the water tank. She waved her blue water bottle in the air. "Liar Grace."

Grace laughed the loudest. Someone threw a scrunched-up piece of paper at her, which struck her on her right temple. She caught the paper before it hit the ground and threw it back. It smacked another girl on the neck.

Aquamarine shook her head. Grace was full of pranks, and now Aquamarine remembered the April Fool's prank she'd played on Kubra two years earlier. Grace had lied that Kubra's father had returned from his Lagos job interview with very urgent news for her. Aquamarine had gone with Kubra to meet him, sympathetic because she, too, shared the pain of a missing parent. Her own father had abandoned the family years before, after claiming he was going to Lagos to find medical help for her sick mother.

During the siesta, the pair hurried to the school gates, only to find Mr. Okorie standing like the Zuma Rock with a long *bulala* in his hand, waiting to accost students who were sneaking into town. He reprimanded the girls for roaming the premises during siesta and for lying to him about a visit from Kubra's father. They barely escaped detention.

Now, while the girls chattered about the old meat sellers and the disappearing students, the mai guardi quietly went into his hut and began to gather his belongings—a green comb, a worn singlet, and his day shoes.

"Mai Guardi," Aquamarine said, "I am sure tomorrow night you will have a more peaceful watch."

"No tomorrow night, Little Miss." He looked past Aquamarine and cast a worried gaze at the huge baobab tree. "I leave today." His voice was shaking.

"*Haba*, Mai Guardi," said Aquamarine. "Because of a vision or a trance or a dream and on and on?"

He nodded, and Aquamarine noticed a dark damp patch on the inseam of his brown pants.

"How will you feed your family, pay your daughter's tuition if you leave your job?" she asked. His daughter, Asabe, had just finished seventh grade at the school.

"Money will come," he said. "But life—only one."

Aquamarine stayed silent, only nodding in return.

"Mai Guardi," Grace said with mock seriousness, "please, come and show us where the girls disappeared before they reappeared at the top of the tree." Her voice was about to crack with laughter.

Earnestly, without smiling, the mai guardi stumped off toward the baobab tree. As Aquamarine and the other girls followed him, past the back of the Red House, past the back of the Blue House, past the clotheslines and the outhouse, he poured out a stream of curses on the bottle for betraying him. He stopped at the barbed-wire fence separating the girls' dormitories from the sports field. The baobab tree stood at the edge of this field; beyond this perimeter, a wooded area led to the school farms. The tree was about forty feet tall, but that was not uncommon. There were lots of similar trees in this newly settled area, and no one had to look far to find snakes and other reptiles. What set the baobab apart was the huge beehive hanging from a branch, so shielded by thick leaves that many of the girls had never noticed it.

"Honey!" Grace squealed.

Asmau looked at the mai guardi. "Are you sure it wasn't a swarm of bees you saw last night?"

"No," he said. "In fact, now I remember. There was also a big, big fire burning in the tree."

Aquamarine and the other girls peered at the baobab. There was no trace of char or ash, no wilted leaves, no scent of smoke. All they saw were bees, flying in and out of their home, making honey.

As Asmau peppered the mai guardi with questions, Aquamarine spotted a chameleon on the fence. It was about four inches long and metallic grey, the same color as the fence. She broke a sprig from the hibiscus that straddled the fence, carefully picked up the chameleon, and placed it on the sprig. Four girls gathered around her, staring in awe at the animal. It stood so still, its eyes unblinking. Then its bumpy skin and eyes gradually transformed, taking on the color and pattern of their red-and-white-checked day uniforms. Aquamarine admired the chameleon's patterned face and bubble eyes. She caressed the air above its head and babble-talked to it.

Grace's voice zoomed into her awareness: "We could make a fortune by selling all that honey." The girls all looked in Grace's direction. Before anyone could cry, "No!" she had picked up a stone and thrown it at the hive. The stone smashed into the side of the nest, then dropped to the ground along with a small chunk of honeycomb. Honey dripped. Bees billowed out of their home, and a mass of insects darkened the sky. Yelping and howling, the girls raced for their dormitories or just the nearest door. A few girls must have been stung: their sharp cries lacerated the air. Aquamarine, running, had just passed the clotheslines when she tripped on a stone and fell face down. Her chin scratched against the sand. Someone's flip-flops clomped on her right shoulder and arm, and quickly a mass of bees encircled her. Jumping up, she flailed and beat at the bees; she ran like a crazy person to the first escape hatch she could find, a door into the Blue House, and banged hard.

"Open the door," she screamed. There was fire on her right shin, fire on her head. Someone opened the door, and hands dragged her into the room.

As Aquamarine stood under a creaking ceiling fan, Asmau quickly pulled out the stings and dabbed her swollen skin with laundry bluing diluted in water.

Once she had recovered a little, Aquamarine thanked the girls and crossed from their dormitory to her own through a connecting door. She went straight to her corner of the room and found Grace lying on her own bed. Grace's lips were quadruple their normal size and marked with laundry bluing. Her left ear, a finger, and a temple were all tinted blue as well. She was scowling.

Just before the 1 p.m. lunch bell, Asmau found Aquamarine and told her that the mai guardi had left for good, right after the bee incident. "The principal should have sacked him a long time ago without any benefits," Asmau said, and sighed. Her thin cheeks became even thinner as she let out her breath.

Aquamarine didn't express her disagreement. She wished the mai guardi well. She only said, "The school has no excuse for continuing to expose us to danger by hiring cheap security." She chose her words carefully, bearing in mind that the principal was Asmau's clanswoman.

"Sure," Asmau said. "I will let you know when a new security guard is hired." She hastened away.

In her locker, Aquamarine found her plate and fork and took them to the dining hall for lunch. She knew her subtle message would reach the right ears, but that didn't mean the right measures would be taken. She wished Kubra's mother was still working at the school. She had always been vocal about issues of student safety.

Aquamarine recalled a time in late January, a few minutes past midnight, when she had accompanied Safiya to the outhouse. Safiya was suffering from a case of mild food poisoning, and Aquamarine waited outside for her with a lantern in hand. To her horror, she saw two silhouetted orbs on the perimeter fence morph into two lurking men. She quickly turned out her lantern and crouched down. The men sat still, scanning the dormitories. When their gaze veered away from her direction, she yelled, "Thief! Thief!" The men vaulted over the fence and fled.

She and Safiya reported the incident to school authorities the following day. Kubra's mother wanted the administration to bring in soldiers to guard the school and asked that the matter be investigated by the Department of State Services, given the increasing terror attacks in the region. But the principal simply asked two local policemen to patrol the premises and keep watch alongside the mai guardi. "Only two policemen and one old mai guardi to protect all the girls in this school, Ma?" Aquamarine had asked the principal.

"There is no cause for alarm," the principal had replied. "You girls should not be afraid. Those men were probably hungry thieves who won't bother your dormitories again, especially with the armed policemen on the grounds."

Aquamarine sat in the far corner of the dining hall. The seats that Grace, Gaddo, and Safiya usually took beside her were empty. None were in the mood to leave the dormitory after the bee attack. She forked a mouthful of *eba* dipped in *egusi* soup into her mouth. A little more salt was needed, as usual. She swallowed and eyed the diced beef coated with whitish paste in her plate. Auntie Ijeoma's *egusi* soups were tastier, usually dotted with chopped green *ugu* leaves. Yet Aquamarine preferred this tasteless soup because, while she ate, no one hovered around her to see if she had stolen an extra piece of meat from the tureen. Thinking back to what she had discovered earlier, she felt disturbed at the thought that Auntie Ijeoma might have written the letter supposedly from Enugu.

Waking from an afternoon nap that had spilled into the early evening, Aquamarine patted the sting on her head and realized that the swelling had reduced considerably. The bump on her shin had dissolved, leaving an uneven indigo patch that she wanted to wash off before even more of it rubbed off onto her green and white polka-dotted bedsheet.

She went outside to the clothesline to collect her towel. Clothes lay strewn on the ground, probably pulled down as students were fleeing the bees. She found her yellow towel twisted into a lump at the foot of a clothes pole. And just a step ahead lay the chameleon. Its head was a crushed mess of blood and sand, bone and brain matter. Its mangled green skin was coated in red laterite sand; its hind feet, rump, and tail hung drooping. Large flies were perched on it. Aquamarine was sorry she hadn't just left the chameleon on the fence. *Perhaps it would still be alive,* she thought.

She wanted to bury the chameleon. As she walked back to her dormitory to find a hoe, she couldn't get the image of its checkered face and eyes out of her mind. The loss reminded her of another lost face—her mother's. On the day Auntie Ijeoma, her mother's younger sister, had arrived in Enugu, prepared to take Aquamarine north to Kasar Lafiya, her mother had sat beside her on her bed. Only the left side of her mother's face had moved when she spoke, slurring her words: "*Aqua m ji n'anya, aga m eleta gị*—My cherished Aqua, I will visit you." That had been ten years ago. Last December, when Aquamarine had again asked Auntie Ijeoma about her mother, her auntie had called her ungrateful and asked if she wanted to go back to disease and death. Aquamarine had decided then that she would write her mother a letter when the new term began in January and tell her she wanted to come home to her.

Aquamarine found her hoe in the box room and went outside again. She buried the chameleon behind the outhouse. Soon, she imagined, wild yellow azaleas would sprout from its grave and mingle with the surrounding flowers. Soon. Then she went and had a bath.

It was about midday, two days later, when Asmau told Aquamarine and her friends that the school had hired a temporary guard named Dogo. Aquamarine wondered if the security situation would really improve with Dogo, and if the other girls shared her worry. But only Grace responded to Asmau, teasing, "Is our new mai guardi also a seer?"

The girls didn't go to the dining hall for lunch that afternoon. One of the joys of their school's extension period was that their time was their own. They were free to prepare for their exams however they chose. Aquamarine wanted to study computer engineering at the University of Nigeria Nsukka, closer to her mother's home, and become a professor. Grace wanted to be a physical education teacher. Gaddo wanted to become a math teacher. Safiya wanted to become a health educator. Today they all sat in Aquamarine's corner of the dormitory, eating *kuli-kuli* and soaked *garri,* then slaving away at algebra and calculus until dinner at six o'clock.

A week later, Aquamarine was bringing in her washed and sundried clothes from the line. The rays of the setting sun cast slanted flaming bars across everything they touched in the dormitory room—over Aquamarine's khaki suitcase at the foot of her bunk, over the gray concrete floors. She folded her clean clothes—her spare day wear, her uniform, and her spare bedsheet—and placed them inside her suitcase. She noticed that the black netting of the mesh bag made tiny *X*-shaped shadows all over the white envelope that contained her mother's letter; they looked like check boxes on a form. Her gaze lingered on the envelope for a moment. She knew the words in the letter had certainly not changed, and sighed.

"Aquamarine," Grace called from her bed, "what kind of sigh is that?"

Aquamarine sighed again. "It's that letter from my mother. I know you all have been waiting for me to tell you something about it."

Grace dropped *Purple Hibiscus,* a book she was reading for her English literature exam, and sat up. "We guessed the letter must contain bad news. Safiya said we should pretend that it didn't exist until you were ready to talk about it. But I've been dying to know what it says."

Aquamarine handed Grace the letter, and then gave her the market list.

"God forbid," said Grace, comparing the two. "Is this letter from the right address? Safiya, Gaddo, come tell me I don't need eyeglasses."

Gaddo and Safiya came over from their corners and pored over the letter and the list.

In the past, all of the girls had shared bits of their lives with one another. Grace had told them about her strong bond with her two younger brothers, how she hoped to marry a man who loved sports, especially soccer. Safiya had admitted that she feared that her mother might be her sister and told them that she had liked the feeling of her family friend Lukeman's soft damp palms when they had shaken hands in the car park before the beginning of term. Gaddo had recounted that her father had betrothed her at birth to a man who was older than her grandfather, in exchange for a few bags of pepper, rice, and beans. He had planned to marry her off at nine years old, but her mother had paid off the debt to the old man with proceeds from her tailoring business. She had then divorced her father, and the pair had fled from Kaduna to Kasar Lafiya. Now Gaddo never wanted to get married.

The girls knew a few things about Aquamarine's past too. She had related how her mother, once a lively teacher and headmistress, had suffered a major stroke; how her father had promised to go to Lagos in search of money and medical help but had never returned; how her auntie had brought her to Kasar Lafiya and now wouldn't answer her when she asked after her mother. They knew she feared that her mother was dead, and they understood that this letter from her mother was momentous.

The girls remained together in Aquamarine's corner of the room, chattering long after lights out. Grace said she had a strong feeling that the letter and the list had been written by the same person—the wicked auntie. "That woman just wants you to continue being her house slave forever," she said.

"Maybe your mother and auntie just write the same way," said Gaddo. "Siblings sometimes have similar handwriting." She told them about her little cousin Amina, such an annoying, adorable copycat. Handwriting was the least important issue on that list of imitations.

"Don't forget, there are people who forge signatures and handwriting for gain," Safiya said, and suggested that they should look at the sender's address on the envelope.

But when Aquamarine showed them the envelope, they saw that the letter had no sender's address, and the postage-stamp ink was faint. Did the last two letters of the stamp read *gu* for Enugu or *ya* for Kasar Lafiya?

"I am going to go to Enugu right after writing my last exam on June 11," said Aquamarine suddenly.

"What if your mother really sent the letter, and she doesn't want to have anything to do with you?" Safiya said.

"That's harsh, Safiya," said Gaddo.

"You have to be prepared for anything. Reality can bite wickedly sometimes," said Safiya.

Aquamarine knew about Safiya's complicated family tree, so she merely said, "In that case, my mother would have to look into my eyes and tell me why she doesn't want me." Her voice sounded more confident than she felt.

"I support you," said Grace.

"Why don't we go to the post office tomorrow and see if we can find out anything about the sender?" Gaddo said. "That might be a good starting point."

Grace and Safiya agreed. Aquamarine nodded. She folded the letter and the list and put them back inside the envelope.

At nine o'clock the next morning, the four girls headed to the post office, which was in the administrative block, nestled between the typist's office and the main office. Aquamarine showed the envelope to Mr. Titus, the postmaster, and asked if he had any record of the sender's address or if he could tell by the stamp from where the letter had come.

Mr. Titus looked through his notebook and announced, "The letter is from Abakpa Crescent, Enugu."

Aquamarine felt both glad and alarmed to learn that the letter might have actually been penned by her mother. How would she be received if she disregarded the note's stern warning and showed up at Enugu? How would she react if she faced rejection again?

"And there is a phone number," Mr. Titus continued. He scribbled it onto a page of his notebook, tore out the page, and handed it to Aquamarine.

Aquamarine noted that the number wasn't one of Auntie Ijeoma's.

Grace offered her phone to Aquamarine. "There's only one way to find out who's behind all this."

Aquamarine took the phone. She felt an adrenalin rush, that kind that usually came when she was seated in an examination hall, ready to write, until her mind suddenly went blank. She dialed the number.

A man with a mellow voice answered, identifying himself as Mr. Cosmas Ahia. Aquamarine's father.

"Papa?" Aquamarine asked. Immediately she wanted to take the word back. She did not think he deserved to be called *Papa*. She hardly knew him. And all she could remember about him was his abandonment.

"*Chei!*" he said. "*Aqua nwa m nwanyi*, how are you?"

"I am fine," Aquamarine said. A glow lit up in her heart as she heard the familiar endearment. When she was little, the name had made her feel special, as if the two had shared an unbreakable bond. The words meant that he acknowledged her as *his* daughter and that made her feel important to him. But then she recalled how he had left her mother, and she doused the sudden warmth.

She wanted to ask, "Papa, where have you been? Why did you say you were going to look for money for Mama's health bills and then for months nobody saw you? What were you doing while you were away? Did you know, at the sound of every car or bus that stopped in front of our house, Mama used to send me to the porch to check if you had come home, until she gave up hope of your returning? Did you know Mama used to murmur, '*Dim*—my husband,' as she slept? Where were you when Auntie Ijeoma came and took me to Kasar Lafiya? And why have you come back?" Instead, she said, "Put Mama on the phone. I want to talk to her."

"Your mother is asleep," he said. Aquamarine did not like the note of finality in his voice. She panicked, suddenly remembering a story in her Christian religious studies class, when Jesus said Lazarus was asleep, yet Lazarus had been dead for four days.

"Is she dead?"

"No," he said.

"Does she have a contagious disease?"

"No. She is fine."

"Can I visit her?"

"I will come and visit you in Kasar Lafiya when you finish your exams in June. Please remain with your auntie."

"Only you? Why won't Mama come with you? Is there something you are hiding from me?"

"We did not expect your mother to survive her illness, and your auntie has contributed so much money toward her medical bills. Money that we cannot pay back."

"And how does that concern me?" Aquamarine asked, and then instantly wished she had framed the question in a way that didn't make her sound rude or indifferent to her mother's predicament.

"*Aqua nwa m nwanyi*, your service to your auntie is a deed of gratitude on our family's part."

"And a repayment of debt?" she said. The endearing name, side by side with the reality of her bonded service to her auntie, felt like mixing bitter medicine with Fanta.

"More like you have saved your mother's life with your service," he said.

She was uncomfortable. His words made her feel like a savior and a slave at the same time, but his reference to her mother made them easier to take. "Are you taking care of Mama?" she asked.

"Yes," he said. "I stopped that *ntakri* phone-card business when I returned to Enugu about ten years ago. I now sell spare parts for vehicles. The work has been slow, but your auntie has been very supportive."

Aquamarine felt like hanging up. She didn't want to congratulate him for finding a better job. Instead, she was crushed to hear that he had returned to her mother just when Auntie Ijeoma had taken her away. And he hadn't even bothered to contact her or make plans to bring her back to Enugu. She was about to press the "end call" button when Grace silently mouthed the words, "Ask him who wrote the letter."

"Can Mama now use her right hand?" Aquamarine asked her father.

"She's learning to use it again."

Aquamarine recalled how her mother had taught her to write an 8, placing her large right hand over Aquamarine's small hand. Together they had drawn one small circle and then another to sit on its head. If her mother was relearning to use her right hand, she wouldn't be capable of reproducing her bold elegant handwriting. "So, who wrote the letter to me?"

"Aquamarine," Mr. Ahia snapped, "are you accusing me of forging your mother's handwriting?"

Aquamarine felt instant remorse at having annoyed him, but she persisted: "Or was it Auntie Ijeoma who wrote the letter?"

"*Mba*!—No!" he said, exasperated. "Your auntie is a generous woman. She pays your school fees, feeds, and clothes you. The least we can do is respect her."

"We?" Would he change his mind if she told him that Auntie Ijeoma weighed the yams, rice, and beans to ensure that her niece hadn't cooked any extra food in her absence? That her auntie counted and recounted the pieces of meat in the stew and soup pots to make sure that not even one could disappear without her knowledge? That her auntie padlocked the refrigerator to see to it that no eatables or drinks were snacked on behind her back? Would he change his mind if he learned about the beatings for little mishaps, the accusations, the suspicions, the unending burden of housework?

"Okay," he said. "The truth is that your mother asked me to help her write the letter."

Aquamarine wondered why he had forged her mother's handwriting and how much "input" her mother had given him. She pointed out, "The letter says that Mama doesn't want me to come to Enugu. Is that your arrangement with Auntie Ijeoma, or is it Mama's wish?"

"Hello?" he said.

"Hello?" Aquamarine said. She was about to repeat her question when she heard her father mumble away from the phone, as though he were speaking to someone else. Then, from a voice softer than her father's, she heard a grunt and a garbled word that sounded like her name.

"Is that Mama?" Aquamarine asked. "Hello? Mama?" But now all she could hear was a dial tone. Somehow she was not surprised that her father had pretended not to understand her question about the letter, and the sound of that garbled voice in the background made her feel as if she were choking. She had to find out if the voice was her mother's.

Panting, Aquamarine dialed the number again, prepared to confront her father as soon as he picked up the phone, but no one answered. She dialed again, and a recorded message unspooled, "The number you have dialed is not available."

Aquamarine handed the phone back to Grace. Through the open door of the post office, she saw the cherry-red blossoms on the lone hibiscus at the center of the square. "I think I just heard my mother's voice," she said sadly. Her eyes itched, and she wanted to cry out with happiness and with misery. Her eyes itched.

Grace, though, shouted for joy and threw her arms around

Aquamarine, then around Safiya and Gaddo. But by the time they were halfway back to their dorm, Aquamarine was in tears.

"Maybe it's not a good idea for me to travel to Enugu," she said. "What if my mother is on my father's and my auntie's side, and she doesn't really want to see me?"

"Let's not assume the worst," said Safiya. "You need to hear your mother's version of the story, from her own lips, before you make a final decision about the truth."

"But I have only 50 naira to spend to get to Enugu," said Aquamarine.

"What do you have us for?" said Grace. And Safiya and Gaddo nodded in agreement.

Grace took charge of the fund drive, going from bunk to bunk to collect. The girls gave donations ranging from 20 to 100 naira. Altogether, she succeeded in raising about 4,500 naira, which would pay for half the fare from Kasar Lafiya to Enugu.

With tears in her eyes, Aquamarine thanked the girls. Her flesh-and-blood family had given her up for money, but her family of friends had given up their own money to help her. "Tears of joy," said the girls, one after the other, patting her on the shoulder as encouragement. But she knew her tears were coming from a place that had nothing to do with joy.

On April 27, Grace received a phone call from her older sister, Helen, who had visited the girls in their dormitory during the previous term. Helen had just spent a month in Damaturu, in neighboring Yobe State, at a month-long National Youth Service Corps orientation camp. Now, with the camp over, the participants would be assigned to posts throughout the country. Helen, who had studied nursing at Bayero University, hoped she would be posted to the Central Hospital in Damaturu.

But after having listened to Helen speak, Grace grumbled, "Only those who know the 'Ogas at the top' get the best postings."

During Helen's last visit to the school, Aquamarine had asked for her advice. At fifteen going on sixteen, she had not yet developed breasts and had never menstruated. Back in ninth grade, eager to fit in, she had bought herself a padded underwire bra and had stuffed it with crumpled paper. But then, during that year's inter-house sports competition she made a big mistake: after winning the junior 400-meter relay race with her teammates, she wore her breasts and bra for the 200-meter race. When she ran through the tape at the finish line, the paper balls fell out of her jersey, and she became known as "Aquamarine, golden girl, paper breasts." Helen, though, had offered comfort: "Have patience. The signs of womanhood will come when they will come."

Like a big sister, Helen usually spoke to all four girls on speakerphone after finishing her private chat with Grace. She told them she had been posted to Gujba College to work in its dispensary unit. The college was only a two-hour journey from Damaturu, but Aquamarine heard worry in her voice.

"Are you concerned about the gunmen who attacked the men's dormitory a few years ago?" she asked.

Helen sighed. "Nowhere is really safe. Even the Central Hospital at Damuturu was attacked that year."

She changed the subject. "I hope you girls are studying hard."

"We are," they said in unison.

"All right, then," Helen said. "My bus is about to set off for Gujba. I'll call again when I reach there."

"Safe trip!" Aquamarine said along with the other girls. They were all smiles.

"Good luck on your exams!"

"Thank you!"

At six o'clock the next morning, Grace phoned Helen. Instead of her sister, a man with a gruff voice answered the call. "God is the greatest!" he shouted, then ranted something in what might have been Arabic. Grace heard the rattle of gunshots in the background.

She ate no food at all that day. She just wept.

"Maybe Helen lost her phone on the bus," Aquamarine said after dinner, pushing a plate of red yam pottage toward Grace. "You should eat something."

Grace shook her head, then sat up and wiped her cheeks with the back of her hands.

Aquamarine set the plate on the bed beside Grace. "Once Helen settles down at her post, she'll find another phone and call you."

Safiya fiddled with her pocket radio, flipping from station to station. "If there was news of an attack, one of the radio stations would be carrying it by now."

"We're talking about a remote village in Yobe State," said Grace.

"If you are worried about an abduction, my little cousin Amina was kidnapped in January, and she escaped," said Gaddo. "Now she's back home with her parents in Tsakiya."

"How is she?" said Aquamarine.

"Pregnant." Gaddo sighed, acknowledging the shock on the other girls' faces.

"Didn't you say she's only thirteen?" asked Safiya.

Gaddo nodded. "My mother hasn't told me the details of her escape, but I'll find out when we visit them in Tsakiya after my exams."

"Let's hope for the best for Helen," Aquamarine said.

Aquamarine hoped their encouraging words would lodge inside Grace's heart and build strength. Yet she felt so hopeless, even more so when her thoughts drifted to her mother. The thought of facing her mother felt like diving off a cliff. What would be at the bottom—hard ground or water?

After lights out, each girl lay in her own bed. Eventually Aquamarine heard Grace's sniffling shift to become a slight snore, and then she let go of her vigilance, turned onto her side, and slept. But about an hour later, Safiya's voice woke her.

"Aquamarine! Aquamarine!"

Aquamarine opened her eyes and saw Safiya kneeling by her bed, her eyes wide with fear.

"There are soldiers in our dorm," she said.

"Soldiers?" Aquamarine jerked to a sitting position. Grace was already out of bed, hurrying to pack whatever she could. All of the other girls in the room were also packing and whispering. Someone was whimpering in the far corner.

"Are we in trouble?" Aquamarine said.

"They said they came to protect us from terrorists," said Safiya.

"Terrorists?" Aquamarine jumped to her feet and dashed toward the door, but Safiya grabbed her arm and pulled her back. She shoved Aquamarine's day wear into her hands.

"You'd better get dressed," Safiya said. "They said we should all get dressed but shouldn't pack anything, not even our phones."

"What kind of instruction is that?" Grace asked. "I won't go anywhere without my phone." She punched a number on her phone, listened for a dial tone, and sighed. "No network in town to reach my father."

"Where do they want to take us?" Aquamarine pulled her day wear over her nightdress and knotted her wrapper around her waist.

"They haven't said," Safiya said under her breath.

Beneath her day wear Safiya was wearing a flowing blouse and a wrapper. She clutched a small blue New Testament to her chest. Aquamarine noticed a bulge above Safiya's stomach. She didn't ask what it was, but the squarish shape reminded her of a diary. At Safiya's side, a curved bulge resembled the hilt of a cutlass for cutting grass. Aquamarine opened her suitcase and snatched out her mother's letter, the piece of paper with her father's phone number, along with a blue pen. She saw the wad of money, raised by her friends for her trip, and thought out loud if she should give it back to the contributors. Grace said no: "You might really need that money along the way."

So Aquamarine stuffed it inside the envelope, wrapped the parcel in a black plastic bag, and carefully tucked the bundle underneath her clothes, wedging it against the belt of her day wear and the knot of her wrapper. "What did you pack?" she asked Gaddo.

"A hoe," Gaddo said.

Aquamarine was shocked. A hoe?

"We can't really trust these men." Grace sneered. "My father, based on his vigilante work experience, said that sometimes the terrorists pretend to be pastors, evangelists, and soldiers, and then without warning they'd attack their innocent victims. Remember what happened at Chibok and other villages in years past."

Aquamarine nodded. She felt a sudden tightness in her chest and fixed her eyes on the door. She didn't know what awaited them beyond that gray wooden door.

Then Grace handed her a little plastic bag.

"Thanks," Aquamarine said, noting her green toothbrush, her red plastic toothpaste tube, a bar of soap, her yellow face towel, and a relay baton with iron rings at both ends. Aquamarine smiled and nodded. She remembered their past chats about how a toy could become a weapon.

Grace was now sitting quietly at the foot of her bed. Her eyes were red and swollen, probably from her tears over Helen, Aquamarine thought. Yet she seemed to be in that focused condition that athletes tap into just before a race begins, just before the referee says, "Go!" Under the *atampa* wrapper tied around her waist she wore a pair of black jeans. Her sneakers were gray. Her black t-shirt was emblazoned with the pop singer Rihanna's smiling face.

Aquamarine fished her sandals from underneath her bed and slipped her feet into them. "Where are they taking us?" she asked.

Before Safiya or Grace could answer, someone kicked open the door. Four uniformed men armed with AK-47 rifles burst in.

"Hurry," said the lankiest of them. He looked like the youngest, too, and he had a hooked nose. "We have to leave now."

The girls hurried out. By the fence stood about three dozen scraggly men. Real soldiers wouldn't look so shabby, Aquamarine thought. Even though the men were armed, she believed the eighty girls had a chance to turn their toys to weapons and run the men out of their school. A beefy man who seemed like their leader began to speak. Then a girl standing behind Aquamarine let out a loud hoot, and all of the girls began to screech and wail, imitating police sirens. As the men blinked, the girls produced their various "weapons" and sprang at them. With her baton Aquamarine struck the head of the man closest to her. Other girls were armed with heeled shoes, hoes, sneakers, canvases, dictionaries, javelins, skipping ropes, and stones, lots of stones from the flower beds that surrounded the dormitories. It was exhilarating to watch the men flee, and the girls jeered at seeing them jump the fences and run toward the gates.

The girls felt victorious. They congratulated each other's bravery and described their own blows. Yet Aquamarine and a few others remained worried: Dogo, their new mai guardi, was missing from his post. Several tried to phone their families—among them, Grace. But when she dialed her father's number, she could not get through. Another girl tried to call her uncle, a policeman, but again there was no reception. Asmau tried to reach the principal, without success.

The girls began to debate among themselves, trying to figure out their best move. Should they walk into town? What was wrong with the phone network? Had the townspeople vanished? As they talked, a girl called their attention to bright lights suddenly beaming beyond the fence, accompanied by the roar of vehicles. Within moments, hordes of men were jumping over the fence into the compound, so many, so fast that they seemed to have appeared out of thin air. The girls had not been victorious after all.

Aquamarine's hand shook as she gripped her baton. Beside the cluster of trees lining the path to the dormitories, three trucks materialized, along with numbers of motorcycles, buzzing like wasps. How did they get in? And where was Dogo? A line of rough-looking men, all in army uniforms, sat on the wall beside the guard hut, in the same place where Aquamarine had glimpsed the two intruders, months before. A man with a long beard strode up to the girls and cleared his throat to speak. As he paused, Aquamarine noticed the feet of the men standing behind him. Some wore black boots, some flip-flops; many were scarred and bare. Clearly, the real Nigerian soldiers were miles away.

"You will come with us," said the bearded man.

For a few seconds the girls remained silent. Then cries, curses, and invocations broke out among the group. Aquamarine did not make a sound. She wanted to shout, "Kidnappers! Kidnappers!" She wanted to re-create her small victory over the two intruders months before; she wanted to reprise their brave battle earlier that night. But now the girls were surrounded by at least three hundred men, and the sheer number made her feel dizzy. Even if they could summon the courage to fight, how would their bowls, buckets, mosquito nets, hoes, batons, and knives stand up to the kidnappers' assault rifles? The cool April breeze blew the rank smell of the men toward her. She knew what became of women and girls abducted by such scoundrels. She thought of her mother and brushed her hand over the small bulge against her stomach. The plastic bag was plastered to her skin with sweat. *They can't steal my dream. I'll see my mother again,* she thought.

Aquamarine turned and saw tears glistening on Grace's cheeks. "These must be the men who killed Helen," she murmured.

Aquamarine whispered reassuringly, "We can't be sure that Helen is dead. Don't give up hope. The men are probably from different groups."

She looked at the commander, then took a deep breath and spoke. "You are strangers," she said. Her voice quavered. "We will not go with you."

"No!" shouted Grace. "We will not go with you!"

Quickly, with Aquamarine and Grace in the lead, the girls spun the words into a chant: "We will not go with you! We will not go with you!"

The commander lifted his rifle and rattled a string of gunshots into the sky. The girls fell silent.

"You better come with us," he said.

Without warning Jemimah and a few other girls broke into a run, but another round of gunshots in the air stopped them in their tracks. Aquamarine glanced at Safiya, who stood next to her. Safiya had not uttered a word since the commander had stepped forward. Aquamarine wanted to give her a nudge, but then Gaddo threw herself to the ground and started pounding the sand with her fists, imploring the earth to open up and swallow her. The hook-nosed soldier who had spoken to them inside their dorm slung down his rifle, grabbed her by the arms, and yanked her to her feet.

"You won't be hurt if you do as I say," he said to her in a low tone.

With his rifle the commander pointed to the nearest truck and ordered, "*Yarinya, tafi.*"

Asmau was the first girl to climb in, and other girls followed her. Aquamarine trudged toward another truck; it, too, was filling fast. The walk to the truck was short, but the weariness in her heart made the trek seem long and laborious, as if she were trudging to the Gwagwalala market on one of Auntie Ijeoma's errands. The air was heavy with the smell of petrol. She repressed the urge to throw up. Behind her, Grace pinched her elbow and whispered, "We have to find a way to escape."

"These men are armed," Aquamarine whispered back.

"I know," murmured Grace. "But sit at the side."

Aquamarine nodded and climbed in. She felt Grace swing in after her and saw her edge her way to Gaddo's side in the corner.

Turning around, Aquamarine found Safiya and stretched out a hand to hoist her up. Safiya whispered that her stomach was rumbling as the two worked their way toward Gaddo and Grace.

An engine roared to life, and Aquamarine felt the truck rock forward. Then she saw that all the buildings in the school were ablaze: the dormitories, the classroom blocks, the dining hall, the school store, the post office, the administration block, the kitchen, the laboratories, the guard hut, the outhouse. The fires leaped high, but the baobab tree loomed above them, silhouetted in the black smoke. Aquamarine watched another dark cloud, the bees, swirl away from the smoke, from their honey, their hive, their home. The drunken mai guardi's words came into her head: "None of the students who went to that market returned."

The truck picked up speed and rumbled through the gates and onto the highway. Looking over the edge, Aquamarine saw the bodies of two policemen, once posted as school guards, lying along the path.

The trucks were the kind used to transport cattle from the northern fields to the southern markets. But these were headed in the opposite direction, packed with girls like sardines in a can. The bed of Aquamarine's still smelled of dung and urine, and now, to add to the misery, many girls were vomiting. Aquamarine felt sick, too, but kept herself from retching. All around her girls were crying, cursing their abductors, yelling for help. Others were frozen in silence. Still others were praying that the rest of the convoy would continue to lag behind. They were watching their chance, hoping to jump out of the truck.

After what seemed like an hour, two girls jumped. Then a third jumped, but she must have broken a bone when she hit the ground because she shrieked so loudly that the others feared the men in the cab had heard her. After waiting for a while, two more girls jumped. Now Aquamarine watched Grace struggle to her feet, and she did the same. She urged Safiya and Gaddo to join them, but neither moved. Safiya whispered that she was afraid of hitting her head on the tar and cracking her skull. Gaddo was frightened of getting squashed underneath the giant tires.

"We have to make an effort!" insisted Aquamarine and was glad to see the two wriggle to their feet.

"The real soldiers will rescue us once our families tell them we have been kidnapped," whispered Gaddo.

Grace shook her head. "The gunmen must have raided the town, too," she said. "Why do you think there's no phone network? It might be a long time before any rescue mission comes looking for us."

"I'm very scared," said Safiya.

Aquamarine longed for magical powers. She wanted to whisk them all away to safety. But she had to jump; she didn't think she could live with herself if she failed to try. She leaned over the bars of the truck bed. The air was cool and fresh, and the trees along the road looked like shadowy formless monsters.

"We have to jump now," said Grace.

Aquamarine tried to judge how far behind the other trucks and the motorcycles might be. The motorcycles were fast; they could easily swoop up close. Below her the road was a dark abyss, but she knew it was made of asphalt and sand. She brushed a hand over the bulge on her stomach and heard the bag rustle. She watched Grace straddle the edge of the truck and jump, disappearing into the shadows of the monstrous trees. Aquamarine urged Safiya and Gaddo forward, but the two leaned into one another and pressed their foreheads together. They could not leap.

"The army will come for us," said Safiya. Gaddo nodded.

Aquamarine thought they were making a mistake. She said goodbye and shook hands with them. As their hands slipped away from hers, she knew they might never see each other again. Now she turned and faced the blackness. She closed her eyes and mentally pictured her leap. Then she climbed over the edge of the truck and jumped at an angle away from it. Midair, she tucked her arms and legs close to her body and, when she landed, tumbled hard onto her shoulder. The left side of her head banged against the asphalt as she rolled down the road. Pain surged through her body.

For a moment, she lay still, feeling as if all her limbs had fallen off. Then she saw oncoming lights and knew she had to get out of the road or be crushed. She got up onto all fours and crept into the shadows, nestling behind a tree trunk. She watched the trucks and motorcycles growl past. When all was quiet again, she began to move, but then a wiry grip clutched her left shoulder.

"*Ke, Yarinya!*" said a surly voice, and a man flashed a torch in her face.

Aquamarine tried to fight off the hand, but he grabbed her roughly. Then the headlights of two motorcycles flashed on, and she saw she was surrounded by four men. Quickly two of them hustled her onto a motorcycle, sandwiched her between them, and sped away after the trucks. Her head was spinning; but just as the motorcycle was catching up with the trucks, she glimpsed a girl dressed in a red jersey and a white skirt, the outfit that her team usually wore for sports competitions. The girl was standing beside a giant tree, waving and calling Aquamarine's name. She wondered why the girl wasn't hiding from the abductors. She wanted to shout, "Run away!" but feared that any sound would endanger the girl. She glanced over her shoulder to see if the man behind her had noticed the girl, and his stony gaze made her shiver. She averted her gaze and fixed her eyes on the road ahead.

Suddenly, out of nowhere, the girl in the red jersey reappeared, now in the path of the motorcycle. She was flagging it down, trying to make it stop.

"Don't kill her! Can't you see her?" Aquamarine yelled, frantically pounding the driver's back with her fists, begging him to stop. The man behind her screamed obscenities and struggled to keep her from toppling the machine. The driver never flinched. He raced straight through the girl on the road as if she were air. To Aquamarine's amazement, there was no massive collision, no shattering of bones or spilling of blood. Then she caught sight of the girl again, standing whole and unhurt on the roadside. Those familiar hawklike eyebrows, that mournful frown. It was Kubra. Kubra's ghost. A ghost. Her head throbbing, Aquamarine passed out.

GADDO'S COUSIN

It was mid-August, and in Tsakiya the sky wept almost every day. Amina was seated at her spot at the dining table, which had room for four, though there were only three in her family. Her father slid his white brocade cap off his head, pushed it down into a corner of his seat, bowed his head, and began to say grace before breakfast. Her hands in her lap, Amina planted her eyes on the *C*-shaped scar on her left wrist and listened to his recitation. Her mother and father chorused "Amen" when he was through. The splatter of rain against the aluminum roof almost drowned their voices. Amina did not speak, though she looked up when he finished and nodded at her parents with a dry smile. Her own *Amen* remained bundled in her heart, along with a secret—this was the day she planned to take her life and that of the baby in her womb.

As they ate bread and boiled eggs and drank their tea, Amina's father talked of the American journalists who, the day before, had visited the Tsakiya town council, where he worked as a clerk. He said that they planned to spend a week in the town, interviewing people about their abduction experiences.

"When I get to the office, I'll make an appointment for Amina for tomorrow morning," said her father.

"Good idea," her mother said.

Her father nodded, licked the breadcrumbs from his thick brown lips, and continued planning for the interview.

Amina looked at her parents, who were talking as if she were not seated with them at the table. Why didn't they ask if she wanted to tell her story to the world? *What view will the world have of me, especially when neighbors gossip about me and say I am a terrorist's wife and my unborn child is spoiled with terrorist blood?* she thought.

She picked up a slice of bread and tore it into bite-sized pieces. Her mother looked over and quickly offered to cut up the other slices on Amina's plate, but her daughter gave her a black look. She had not gotten over the fact that her mother wouldn't let her have her own knife at the table. No doubt, her mother feared that Amina would make another attempt to slash her wrist, as she had done three months earlier. But now Amina had a better weapon. The night before, her mother had forgotten to lock up the mosquito insecticide in the store cabinet. Amina had sneaked the half-empty can into her school bag and hidden it in her wardrobe. After breakfast her parents would leave for work, and then she would drink it.

As Amina chewed her bread, she fixed her gaze on the blue china fruit bowl at the center of the table. The bowl's glaze rippled with a thousand spidery cracks.

Amina was thirteen years old, but since her return from captivity, her parents had made all decisions for her, as if she were an infant or had lost her mind. When the doctor had warned that an abortion was too risky, they had announced that they would care for her child until she had completed her education and become independent. They hadn't bothered to ask Amina if she wanted anything to do with the child, given how it had been fathered. They hadn't asked if she wanted to live with the trauma, the shame, and the torment.

Amina blinked and swallowed hard as thoughts of the day of her abduction flared into her mind.

GADDO'S COUSIN

On that Monday morning, the January harmattan haze had reduced visibility to about ten huts away. She was preparing to return to school for the new term and was eagerly anticipating the mock exams for the junior secondary school certificate, scheduled for the end of term. But before leaving for school, she had to help her mother fill the water barrel in the kitchen. The community well was close to a stretch of farmlands that lay beyond the health center. She walked out with her *guga*, its long rope neatly rolled up and stuffed inside the small plastic pail, and found that the well, for the moment, was deserted. And that was when a middle-aged man appeared from the haze with a machete in his hand.

"If you scream, you are dead," the man said. He had a wild look in his eyes, and though he spoke in Hausa, his accent was crude. "You will come with me now."

She stared straight at him. Her heart felt as if it were jumping out of her chest. "Who are you? Why should I go with you?"

The man cursed and said impatiently, "The problem with western education is that girls like you, who should never speak before men, are being trained to ask stupid questions."

As he dropped his eyes from her face to her chest, she flung the guga away, whirled around, and tried to flee, screaming for help. But she got nowhere. Instantly, he hit her in the head with the butt of his machete, and she passed out.

She woke the next day, lying on a torn raffia mat on the floor of a clay hut with a thatched roof. There was no furniture in the room, only a lamp in the corner. She could not remember how she had gotten there. She felt sore all over as though she had been in a wrestling match. Her head ached. She felt moist between her legs and sat up in fright. Had she urinated in her sleep? Her underwear was missing. She touched herself. In the pale lamplight she saw sticky blood on her fingers. She stank. Her dress stank. The room stank. And then she remembered: then it all came back to her, and she knew what her abductor had done. He had told her that he was Ramzi and that she now belonged to him. He boasted that women have their place in this world—under men. Pinning her to the mat, he had driven his message into her pelvis.

And the days had grown into weeks and the weeks into months. She missed her parents, missed school, missed her friends, missed life in Tsakiya Town. She missed her monthly period twice.

Amina snapped out of her thoughts; her mother was calling her name. She looked up and saw curious yet sympathetic eyes.

"Don't you like the food?" her mother said. "Do you want something else for breakfast?"

Amina shook her head. She stared down into her mug and saw a faint reflection of her face on the filmy surface of the tea. There were bags under her eyes and her sadness frightened her.

All this sadness was Ramzi's fault. She remembered sitting on the raffia mat under his roof, suffering from the stench of the filthy toilet pail in the corner. Ramzi's fake Nigerian army uniform, which he sometimes wore on raids with other abductors, lay in a heap. The food he had brought her an hour earlier remained untouched on the floor. The boiled *doya* was as hard as rock. She looked at the plate of stew, at the dull steel fork, its slim prongs partly submerged in tomatoes. The fork reminded her of a silver curtain rod draped with red clumpy curtains. The stew smelled burnt. She had no appetite, and she recalled how her father would bribe her with ice cream to coax her into eating her bean porridge, which she hated with a passion, much to the displeasure of her mother. Despite her misery, the image made her laugh.

Then she heard a key in a padlock. The door creaked open, and Ramzi entered, his face shining like granite in the lamplight. He pulled off his kaftan, flung it and his cap on the ground, and dropped to his knees on the mat. He felt for her breasts, felt between her legs. When she pushed at his hands, he released her, only to grip her throat and squeeze until she was gasping for breath. She had no power to keep him away from her. As he forced her legs apart, sweat rolled from his face and dripped into her eyes. The room was stifling; his flesh was sticky. In her mind was the memory of the big brown entrance door of her parents' house and her mother's black face, warning her, "You must not allow any man to touch you until you are married. The only man permitted to touch you is your husband. Do you hear me?"

On her back Amina reached out and fumbled toward the stew plate on the floor. She found the fork, clutched it in her fist, and stabbed the prongs into Ramzi's throat. He screeched like a wounded animal, instantly he let go of her, arched forward as gouts of blood pumped from his neck, then slumped face down beside her. He twitched and became still.

Amina rolled away from him and stood up. She stared in shock at his body and the widening pool of red. She looked at her hands. They were spattered with blood. She tore off her burka and abaya and used them to wipe her face, her neck, her hands. Then she put on Ramzi's kaftan and cap. She stepped out of the hut, closed the door, and clicked the padlock shut. The fresh air was thrilling, but her heart drummed wildly. She had blood on her hands.

Amina jerked up her head. Her parents had stood up from the table. She hadn't heard the remainder of their discussion. They said their goodbyes and hurried off to work. Amina shut the door after them and, through the window, watched them speed away on her father's motorcycle. She felt a tug of relief: now she had the house to herself. She focused her thoughts on the poison in her wardrobe. She rushed to her room, but as she opened the wardrobe, her phone rang. It was her father, reminding her that he'd cleaned the henhouse in the backyard and encouraging her to get some fresh air. He often made such calls during work hours, checking in to see how she was faring at home.

After hanging up, Amina closed the wardrobe. There was something delicate in her father's voice. Perhaps that delicacy had always been there, but maybe her guilt over her suicide plans had made her take special notice of it today. The care in her father's voice became a rope that pulled her away from the wardrobe and into the backyard.

Amina stood beside the aluminum and wire netting of the chicken house. She took a deep breath. The air smelled heavenly. She watched the chicks pressing their tiny beaks into the fluff of their mother's rich brown feathers. Their small clucking was like music. Amina closed her eyes for a moment and hummed along with them, grateful that her father had taken extra care to keep the house so clean, grateful that he was trying to help her erase the memories of the months in Ramzi's fetid hut. She recalled the dry wind that had whipped against her face and filled her lungs as she'd fled. On that dark night, with only a slim crescent moon in the sky, she had raced through bushes, through forests, as if ten lions were after her. An old couple had directed her to the track that led to Tsakiya and by nightfall of the following day she'd found her way home.

Amina's mother owned a wrapper stall at the market, and after she shut it down for the day she took Amina to her fifth session with Dr. Zainabu Liya, the military trauma specialist at the health center. Amina confessed her suicide plan to them and explained why she hadn't gone through with it.

"This is a forward step in the healing process," Dr. Liya said. "It's good to think about the people who love you and the people you love."

Amina felt a twinge of guilt, but her mother squeezed her hand reassuringly.

"The next step is forgiveness," said Dr. Liya. "You don't have to punish yourself. What happened to you was not your fault."

Amina nodded and blinked back tears.

"Legally, too, you are not at fault," she said. "Killing your attacker was an act of self-defense. So don't allow torment to eat you up. Forgive yourself."

Amina nodded. She was grateful for her mother's hand in hers.

"But most importantly," Dr. Liya said, looking into her eyes, "you need to forgive your abductor. Release from your heart those who have hurt you. Only then will you feel free of this weight and be able to move forward with your life."

Amina stared at Dr. Liya and wondered how she could forgive the man who had violated her. Her palms suddenly felt wet, as though they were bathed with Ramzi's blood, and without thinking she rubbed them together.

After dinner, Amina's mother sat at the foot of her daughter's bed. She said, "It's okay if you don't want to talk to the journalists. I understand that you worry about other people's judgments. But know that your father and I love you no matter what, and we don't want to let you down again."

Amina sat with her back against her bedpost and stared down at the brown satiny hands in her lap.

"But," her mother continued, "I'd like you to think of your cousin Gaddo and the other girls and women who are suffering. Your story could give strength and hope to others."

Amina didn't look up or answer when her mother said good-night. After her mother shut the door, she stretched out on her bed and stared at the dull pink wall through the blackness. She thought about forgiving herself and Ramzi. She thought about her education and her baby. And she thought about Gaddo and Gaddo's mother.

Months back, in late April, they had learned that about eighty girls at the St. Thomas Memorial School in Kasar Lafiya had been abducted. Gaddo was one of them. Her mother, Auntie Uwa, was Amina's mother's first cousin, and she was beside herself with anxiety, so much so that she had developed high blood pressure and was hospitalized in Tuddai, a neighboring village. When Amina and her mother had gone to visit, Auntie Uwa had asked Amina's mother to fetch her a cup of water. As soon as she was out of sight, Auntie Uwa had gripped Amina's hand and riddled her with questions.

"How did you escape? Did someone help you? How did you do it?"

"I killed a man," Amina had said. Auntie Uwa had dropped her hand as though it were made of fire. Amina remembered the tiny black and gray curls escaping from her auntie's black nylon headscarf. She remembered her swollen face, legs, and arms and her panting breath.

"You?" Auntie Uwa laughed. Her puffy eyes strained in her face. "Last Christmas you didn't have the courage to squash the lice in Gaddo's hair. You used to be afraid to stomp on the sugar ants in your mother's kitchen."

Amina nodded, though she wished her auntie would stop.

"Those men who took Gaddo have killed thousands of people," Auntie Uwa said. She stared directly at Amina. "I wish them nothing but torment. Torment is the companion of the blood-guilty."

Amina's palms felt clammy, as if they were still covered in gouts of Ramzi's blood, and she secretly rubbed them on her wrapper.

"What plans do your parents have for the baby?" Auntie Uwa asked.

Amina bit her lip and stared at the tile floor. Her parents had had so many arguments about abortion and the definition of sin, about abortion and adoption.

"Amina?" persisted Auntie Uwa.

"Auntie, they plan to keep the baby and raise it as their own."

She didn't bother to explain that the doctors had said that having an abortion at her age might make it impossible for her to have more children in the future. Sometimes she felt that the baby had no right to exist. She hadn't asked for it. At other times she thought of how faultless the baby was in all of this, but always she would remember how it had been sown, how Ramzi's blood ran in its veins. Like thorns, images of violation would spring into her mind and choke every kind thought in her heart. She longed for the baby to vanish.

Auntie Uwa shook her head. "I hope Gaddo will be strong like you and escape back home."

Amina nodded.

At daybreak, Amina took a bath. By 7 a.m., she was dressed in a sunny yellow wrapper and blouse and had joined her parents at the breakfast table. She munched a mouthful of *masa*. Then, after swallowing, she looked from her mother to her father and said, "I'm ready to tell my story."

When her parents nodded quietly, Amina felt her baby kick.

PART TWO:
2016

KUBRA'S WATCH

Major Danjuma had made his peace with Mother since my death. After she had forbidden him to blame himself, he had begun visiting her every other day, bringing *suya* as he had done in the past and telling Hausa folktales to Danladi.

Now, in his office at the Zone 6 police station in downtown Kasar Lafiya, he sat at his desk with his head in his hands. A February copy of *Watch Magazine: One-Year Anniversary Edition* lay before him, filled with headlines that read:

"SYRIA REFUGEE CRISIS WORSENS: UN Calls for Peace."

"TERROR IN PARIS:
One Year Since Offices of Satirical French Magazine
Attacked by Radicalized Brothers."

"ONE YEAR IN VIEW: LIBBY LANE BECOMES THE CHURCH
OF ENGLAND'S FIRST FEMALE BISHOP AMIDST
DISRUPTIONS FROM PRIESTS YELLING:
'Show where this exists in the Bible.'"

PART TWO: 2016

"THE UN SECURITY COUNCIL, THE P5+1 (FRANCE, CHINA, RUSSIA, THE UNITED KINGDOM, AND THE UNITED STATES, PLUS GERMANY) AND IRAN MEET ON THE IRAN NUCLEAR DEAL."

"THE AFRICAN UNION PLEDGES MORE AID TO NIGERIA'S FIGHT AGAINST TERRORISTS."

In the local news section, the first headlines read:

"PVC/CARD READER CONTROVERSY:
Review of past presidential elections, millions of Nigerians were alleged not to have had PVCs. Impact on the electoral process."

"BIRNIN HASKE SUICIDE BOMBING:
A female suicide bomber, apparently about 10 years old, killed herself and 19 others, possibly against her will, at a market in Birnin Haske."

But one particular headline in the recent news section seemed to have soured Major Danjuma's mood:

"DIKWA SUICIDE BOMBINGS:
Two female suicide bombers detonated themselves in the middle of an internally displaced persons' (IDP) camp. 60 persons dead, another 78 wounded."

Of course, the major could not see me perching on the corner of his desk watching him look at the magazine. There were so many deaths recorded. I was reminded of Auntie Maryam's history class about Egyptian funerary customs. When people died, Ma'at, the goddess of truth and justice, weighed their hearts against a feather of truth, under the inspection of jackal-headed Anubis, the god of embalming, as Thoth, the ibis-headed god of writing, recorded the results. Any heart that was not light enough to go to the afterlife was trapped forever in the underworld or eaten by Ammit, the devourer of the dead. The suicide bombers who believed they were performing good deeds; their victims, the martyrs, who believed they were faithful; the handlers of the suicide bombers, who believed they were doing righteous work: how would they fare with Anubis' scale and scrutiny? *Hauka ne!*—Crazy!

I am still trapped in limbo. But Mother used to tell Danladi and me about Jannah, paradise, the "garden of everlasting bliss," a "home of peace" for those who performed good deeds. That was before she and Father began attending St. John's, the Anglican church in Kasar Lafiya; before Danladi and I began learning about heaven and hell in Sunday school.

Major Danjuma's ringtone jangled: the chorus of Tiwa Savage's track "Standing Ovation," featuring Olamide. His voice was crisp; quickly he hung up, snatched his beret, set it properly on his head, and stormed out the door. He was on a new assignment; and with a couple of other officers, he jumped into a black patrol car and zoomed away.

At the corner of his desk sat Mother's photo in a small silver picture frame. Her smiling face filled the frame. They had met in early 2014 when Mother had gone to the Zone 6 police station to bail out a southern nonacademic junior staff who had been falsely accused of theft of store materials at St. Thomas. Before my death, I had felt that he was planning to ask her to marry him. Our home was like his second home; we always enjoyed the savory *suya* he brought for us every other day, and I always used the tip he gave to help me improve my sprint speed and stamina when I had just turned fifteen and was always hungry: drink plenty of *kunu* and replace the sugar with glucose. But perhaps Mother was holding him off. Perhaps she hoped that Father would crawl out of his hiding place and be reunited with her.

I don't believe I will ever see Father again. And I think Mother is holding on to a dream that will never become real. Father is a deserter.

I should visit her. If I could, I would convince her to move on with her life and forget him.

As I thought of Mother and our house, I found myself floating through its walls into our sitting room. No one was home. Danladi was certainly at school, and Mother was probably visiting or shopping.

I liked that she kept the place tidy. I stood before the cabinet that held my golden trophies and the photos of my friends and me. I remembered their kidnapping and my inability to help them. And I remembered the day when I had asked them about Persephone being kidnapped by Hades. That had been a year before their own kidnapping, and we had all laughed at my silly question. I remembered the icy Fanta that Grace had brought me from the tuck shop, how its penetrating coldness had shocked my broken tooth. Time flies.

GADDO

Erase the screech of chalk on blackboard as Auntie Halimatu solves an algebra equation. Erase the blackboard, the chalk, and Auntie Halimatu. Erase the school buildings and the chattering students and the teachers. Now add a crescent of unwashed angry men in fake Nigerian army uniforms, all of them carrying AK-47s in one hand and rocks as big as kerosene mangoes in the other. Their black boots stamp the yellow-brown sand. Add all of the twelfth-grade girls of St. Thomas Memorial School, minus the lucky escapees. Strike off their happy chatter when the break-time bell rings. Erase the laughter that erupts from the "dynamic four" as they taunt mess-mess queen Grace for polluting the air in her sleep. Add blank stares. Add the glare of the Sahelian midday sun, the slim baobab trees and short jacarandas on the fringes of the clearing, the silent witness of the forest. Keep the beads of sweat on Gaddo's nose. This is that moment.

Gaddo could not sigh; she could not cry. Numbly, she looked at Safiya's head, her yellow scarf. Safiya had been buried alive up to her neck. She looked like a star stuck to the ground. Malam Hamzah, the camp's commander, had warned the girls that anyone who made a scene would suffer the same fate. But what had Safiya done? That mule-faced Asmau, once their classmate and now a camp spy, had told Malam Hamzah's wife, Binta, that, during midday Koran class, she had been reciting the Book of Infidels instead of the Hadith. Binta must have told Malam Hamzah because Malam Hamzah called Safiya an adulteress and subjected her to the *Rajm*.

Gaddo glared at Malam Hamzah. Expressionless, his long beard swaying, he nodded his skull-like head at the men holding stones, and each cast it at the yellow star. The first stone struck Safiya on the forehead with a dull sound, as if she were sack of *bambara* nuts. A bloody stream burst into life, running down her closed eyelids and cheeks, into her mouth, dripping from her chin. The sand licked up the blood as it fell. Under her breath, Gaddo counted the stones: one, two, three, . . . thirty-four in all. Gaddo's husband, hook-nosed Kadir, cast the last one. He had been one of the young abductors who had stormed their hostels the year before. When she could no longer see the yellow star under the mound of stones, Gaddo bowed her head and closed her eyes.

For the entire week that followed, Gaddo wouldn't speak to Kadir. On February 11, she didn't thank him when he gave her a small wooden box of golden Lebanese trinkets. That night, on their mat, as she had done all week, she slept with her back towards him. When his hand mistakenly brushed her shoulder, she swatted it off like a bug. Kadir grunted in pain. *His business!* she thought. Gaddo was sure that if Kadir had really wanted to, he would have already reported her wild reaction against him to Malam Hamzah, and she would have become a second Safiya. She was angry at him, but sometimes she was also thankful. Unlike the other men, Kadir had never beaten or raped his wife. Yet sometimes fear crept into her heart. One day she might push her luck too far.

Gaddo sighed. When Kadir's slight snores returned, she turned onto her back, fixing her eyes on the darkened thatch. Last October, they had married and she had moved into his hut, but he had never tried to kiss her. He had never touched her before or after their marriage. Almost always he started snoring the moment his head touched his pillow.

Till now, it had never crossed her mind to take action against Kadir for being a terrorist. But then he joined the other men to cast stones at Safiya's head, and she had become consumed by wicked thoughts. She could not stop imagining what could happen to someone's head while he slept.

She looked at Kadir in the weak light of the lamp that stood on a stool at the corner. His bushy hair was black. His forehead had fine lines. His brow was marked with a brokenness that he was able to hide during the day, when he was with the other men. She loved the suppleness of his lips, and she aways wondered what they would feel like pressed to hers.

Gaddo closed her eyes and images of Safiya's head filled her memory. She recalled her friend at school, a quiet girl, who had transferred at the start of grade 11 and at first was alone most of the time. Grace was the one who had invited her to join their group of four as they ate the fried *doya* and eggs, and *masa* that Kubra had bought at the town market.

It was Monday afternoon during their midterm break, and all five had stayed at school instead of going home. Together they sat in Aquamarine's and Grace's corner of the dormitory and gossiped about the tension between the school's math teachers, Auntie Halimatu and Mr. Okorie. The pair used to argue in the staff room about how to spark students' love of math via algebra and calculus. In their arguments, Mr. Okorie loved to brandish grandiose mathematical jargon while Auntie Halimatu relied on plain speech. Then, for her birthday, which fell on the last day of class that term, Mr. Okorie gave her his old copy of *The History of the Cartesian Coordinate System: A Very Short Introduction*. She carried it to class without opening it. Then, after writing an in-class assignment on the board, she picked up the book. Out fell an engagement ring, which clanged on the cement floor. Grace, a skilled ventriloquist, began making wedding-bell noises, disguising them behind a plastic smile, and the other students giggled uncontrollably.

But despite the students' enthusiasm, the romance between Mr. Okorie and Auntie Halimatu went nowhere. At the beginning of the new term, rumors spread that Auntie Halimatu had married a man named Alhaji Kontagora over the holidays. Her parents had rejected Mr. Okorie's proposal because he had refused to convert to their Muslim faith, and they had threatened to keep Auntie Halimatu from teaching if she showed any interest in him. Soon the girls learned that the school wanted to hire more teachers from the north and that Mr. Okorie would be sacked to make space for them.

As far as most of the girls knew, interactions between the pair were now limited to Mr. Okorie's "Good morning, Hajia," and Auntie Halimatu's "Good morning, Mr. Okorie." So as Gaddo and the others finished their fried *doya* and eggs and began nibbling on *donkuwa* and *masa,* they were surprised to hear Safiya blurt out that there was more to the story.

On the day school had closed for the midterm break, she had walked into the staff room to return the erasers and chalk and had seen Mr. Okorie and Auntie Halimatu at a desk, holding hands with their foreheads touching as Mr. Okorie spoke tenderly. Quickly, Safiya warned her new friends to keep this a secret: both teachers could lose their lives if Auntie Halimatu's family were to hear such a story. The girls promised, though Grace had joked that math teachers should never be punished for solving circle theorems with their heads and balancing inequalities with their hands. After that day, the four often asked Safiya to hang out with them and talk. But then, a couple of months later, Kubra died.

Touching heads. Tangents and circles. Gaddo looked again at Kadir's head and didn't think she could ever bear its touch, after what he had done to Safiya's. She got up and turned off the lamp, then lay down with her back towards him. But sleep wouldn't come.

Binta had visited their hut the day before Safiya's stoning, part of her weekly routine—checking in on the camp wives and handing out a plate of *tuwo shinkafa* that tasted like water. "A gift of appreciation for the loyalty your husband shows to my husband, our leader, and to our cause," she had said. And then Binta had started wagging her tongue about babies and camp marriage and Kadir and Gaddo's lack of children. Gaddo had responded that she was barren.

That night, after Gaddo told Kadir what she had said, he laughed: "Perhaps she will mind her business next time." But then, the next day, he had joined the other men to stone Safiya. *What could be more complicated than logarithms and exponential functions?* Gaddo pondered. She knew that their marriage would be consummated eventually. It surprised her that Kadir would put up with her stubbornness, and his tolerance made her curious about his thoughts. Why had he never rebuked her? He wasn't even strict about calling her by her new Muslim name, Faizah, and still referred to her as Gaddo.

As Gaddo's eyes became heavy with sleep, random images filled her mind.

Amina.

Gaddo wished she and her mother had visited Amina and her parents before Malam Hamzah and his good-for-nothing men raided their hostel last April. Perhaps she would have known Amina's escape trick and used it to get out of this camp.

Safiya.

Gaddo had admired the steady look in Safiya's eyes, even after the first stone struck. Her eyes didn't cloud with tears. She just stared straight through the men as they hurt her; and when the blood trickled down her face, she closed her eyes. She must have been praying to God to forgive the men for their ignorance, as Stephen did in the Acts of the Apostles, when Saul ordered his stoning.

At school, after Kubra had died and Safiya had won her spot in their sprint team, Safiya would talk passionately to Gaddo and the others about mansions in heaven. Gaddo would always joke that, until she lived in a mansion in Kasar Lafiya, she was not hoping for an invisible one in heaven. Although Gaddo had regularly attended church with her mother, it was simply a social function to her. She loved the bazaars mostly, because there was always lots of food to share and eat and the gatherings gave her a chance to mingle with the other young people in the community. Safiya was different. She believed.

"Gaddo. Gaddo, wake up. Wake up," said Kadir.

Gaddo jerked awake to find his hand gripping and shaking hers. He knelt beside her on the mat, dressed in his fake army uniform. Light poured into the room from the open window. She struggled to keep her eyes open; but when she finally did, he let go of her hand.

"You must have had a bad dream," he said, frowning.

"Dream," Gaddo repeated, still groggy. She remembered every detail of the dream but didn't know what to make of it. In it, her mother had been dead inside a coffin. And when Gaddo went to pay her last respects, her mother's face morphed into Kubra's face. And then Kubra's face morphed into Safiya's face. And then Safiya's face morphed into Kadir's face. And then Gaddo woke up and found Kadir holding her hand, calling her name.

Kadir poured water into a metal cup and gave it to her. Gaddo drank greedily. She eyed his shabby uniform and remembered that he had been wearing it when he had stoned Safiya. She remembered that she had resolved to never speak to him again.

Kadir sat on the low stool by the wall. "What was your dream about? You screamed in your sleep."

Gaddo looked at the wall beside her.

"I know you are angry with me for joining in to kill your friend. Will you forgive me?" he said tensely and let out a sharp breath.

Will forgiveness bring her back from the dead? Gaddo wanted to ask. Instead, she glared at him.

"I'm really sorry," Kadir said.

Gaddo averted her gaze. The earnestness in his eyes was piercing. He didn't look like a radicalized nutcase. Sometimes she wished he would yell at her when she acted out so that she could have more solid reasons to hate him. Yet each day he did the opposite. No other male had ever apologized to her for doing her wrong. And here was this killer-abductor, this man who stood for everything horrifying in the world, apologizing to her when he had every reason not to. Hadn't she tortured him enough with her silence? Even though she had never told him, she'd enjoyed his jokes and the laughter they shared. But that was before he had stoned Safiya.

She looked up at him. She could have told him about the dream, but then she would have had to mention the part about her mother. And seeing her mother lying among her dead friends unsettled her. If she spoke about the dream, it might develop a life of its own and become inevitable. She didn't want to imagine that her mother was dead. She wanted to flush the dream from her memory.

"More water," Gaddo said, and held out her cup to Kadir.

He smiled, his eyes sparkling at the sound of her voice. "Finally, she talks to me." He lifted the jug from the floor and filled her cup.

Gaddo tried not to smile at his delight. She focused on drinking the water, closing her eyes to shut out his intense gaze. The only sounds she heard were the noises in her throat as she gulped.

"Now," said Kadir, "I would nickname you Camel."

Gaddo looked at him over the rim of the cup. A smile played on his lips. He would call her Camel? Was she ugly like a camel in his eyes? If they were giving each other nicknames, she would call him Vulture. Not that he resembled a vulture in any way. He was the handsomest man she had ever met. She would call him that to keep up her pretend dislike of him.

"*Wallahi*," he said. "You are fated to finish the little water we have in this hut."

She tried to suppress a giggle and mistakenly gulped too much water and choked. Still gripping the cup, she thumped her breastbone with her free hand and coughed hard. In an instant, Kadir was kneeling beside her. He took the cup from her, set it down, and held her hand while he gently patted her back.

When Gaddo's cough subsided, she became conscious of the soothing pressure of his hand on hers and could smell his musky scent, his dusty uniform, his fresh sweat. The gaze in his honey-colored eyes was a hook into the depths of her heart.

"Kadir," a man called from outside. "*Zo mu tafi.*"

Gaddo pulled her hand away. He was on his way to another raid, on his way to destroy another village. Yet moments ago that hadn't mattered to her.

Kadir looked at the closed door and shouted, "*Ina zuwa,*" so that the man outside could hear him.

Gaddo was unsure, uneasy. What had she expected, before the man had interrupted them?

Then Kadir whispered, "I will never hurt you. And if you ever want to talk about your dream or anything else, I will be here for you."

He hastened out, shutting the door after himself. Gaddo was upset that he did not cast one last look back at her, as he usually did. She looked at her hand and remembered the warmth she had felt from his. She stared at the door. It was made of eight planks reinforced by rough wooden sticks that formed two cascading Zs. Kadir's spare shirt hung from a nail at the top of the first Z. It reminded her of the night of her abduction. But it also reminded her of his smooth tawny face and expressive eyes. She looked away and sighed. "What am I doing?"

Two days later, when Kadir returned, he immediately lay down on the mat and fell asleep. By midnight, he was shivering, and Gaddo felt heat where his elbow touched her back. She turned over and lay a palm on his forehead. It felt like a steaming hearth. She shook him awake, unbuttoned his shirt, and stripped it off. She poured cool water from the jug into a bowl and used her small towel to wash his body, starting with his face. By the time she reached his torso, the water in the bowl was murky and hot. She opened the door and poured it away, then refreshed it. As she rubbed the towel along his arm, she noticed mosquito bites and bruises. She ran the cool towel over his taut stomach, stopping just before his line of hair thickened and disappeared into his trousers. She noted a flat brown mole she had never seen before. She rolled him over and swabbed his back. By now his temperature was lower, and goose pimples were popping up all over his body. She covered him with one of her light cotton wrappers, and he slept without shivering for the remainder of the night.

The next day, Kadir's temperature was much higher. He was clearly too sick to go raiding with Malam Hamzah and the other men. Gaddo fed him boiled yams and *dogonyaro* leaf tea that she had gotten from Binta. But while she was swabbing him, he vomited up his dinner and began fighting her off.

As his temperature increased, he claimed that black stars were tearing into his flesh and asked Gaddo to give him a razorblade to cut them out.

Gaddo remembered ninth grade, when Grace had malaria. Feverish and hallucinating, she had started punching the air, hitting anyone who came too close. She said the trees were flogging her with their branches, trying to turn her into a tree, and she had to fight them off. The school nurse gave her a round of chloroquine injections, and the fever soon subsided. But when Aquamarine and Kubra asked her about the tree delirium, she told them they were lying. "How can trees walk and talk?" she had said.

Gaddo made up her mind to ask Binta and Malam Hamzah to find a doctor if Kadir's fever continued the next day. But when morning came, the fever had broken. All day he sweated profusely, and his collarbones stood out like cords.

That night he sat on the stool and ate his dinner of boiled black-eyed peas. When Gaddo told him about the black stars and his request for a razorblade, he hooted with laughter. He said his mother used to call malarial high fever "the door between life and death." He recalled, "How people battled the fever determined which side they found themselves on when the door swung shut."

Later that night, as they lay on their mat, Kadir told Gaddo that ever since he had stoned Safiya, he had been dreaming of his mother weeping. Each time, when he would reach out to touch her and ask to help her, she would vanish.

"Where is your mother?" Gaddo said, glad to hear about his family.

"Slaughtered," said Kadir. "They slaughtered my family during a religious riot in Bauchi when I had just turned sixteen in 2009. They didn't think my family was *faithful* enough."

Gaddo lay on her side, watching as he talked. How absurd it was that, in the name of God, the terrorists slaughtered both Christians who worshipped God and Muslims who were not Muslim *enough*. In the end, everyone would face judgment before this same God. She thought of centuries past, all of the purgings based on religion. Would a day ever come when nobody fought the other in the name of God?

"I'm sorry for your troubles," she said.

Kadir smiled wryly. "Life and troubles are two sides of the same coin. I was about to graduate from the Federal Government College in Azare. But my dream of going to the university and becoming a lawyer was crushed." He paused and then said, "I don't believe that killing infidels is the will of God. I don't even believe in God or paradise."

Gaddo thought she hadn't heard him correctly. She leaned in closer and waited to learn where his talk would go.

"My parents were faithful worshippers," said Kadir. "Where was God when the terrorists slaughtered them like cows and forced me to join the raiders? Months ago, we killed dozens of Christian boys. Where was their God to save them?"

"Why do you stay here?" asked Gaddo.

"Apart from the fact that I have no other family to call my own, I think I'm searching for something. The funny thing is, I don't know what it is. But I'm sure I will recognize it when I find it."

"Have you thought of walking away? Starting life someplace else?"

"They'll hunt me down and slaughter me," said Kadir. "I know too much about them. I've been on raids to kill people who tried to escape."

Gaddo noticed that his throat tightened when he said *hunt*.

"Perhaps you're searching for what you lost in your parents."

"Maybe I'm searching for peace. Real peace."

Gaddo wanted to brush away the worry lines spreading across his forehead. Instead, she cupped his bearded chin and turned his face towards hers. Gently she kissed him. His lips were soft, and his beard tickled.

Kadir smiled at her. But when he didn't kiss her back, she felt embarrassed. He would think she was loose, she worried. She rolled over and turned her back to him. Then he threw an arm across her waist and pressed his body against hers. Her heart thumped wildly, joyously, and she smiled to herself. She loved the warmth of his breath against her neck. And she loved that he didn't try to go further. She didn't think she was ready for anything beyond this. For now, she felt safe in his embrace.

When Gaddo woke, Kadir was gone. She knew he had left for a raid in Kasar Lafiya or another town, one that would result in more civilian deaths, but she felt no guilt about desiring him. Her mind went blank when she imagined what she would do if her mother or the parents of any of her friends became one of Kadir's victims.

After attending the afternoon's Koran class under a giant dadawa tree, Gaddo was walking back to her hut when she saw Aquamarine surrounded by Asmau, Binta, Malam Hamzah, and Ahmad, a scruffy middle-aged man who was one of Malam Hamzah's commandants. Gaddo drew closer to the group and heard Malam Hamzah discussing his plan to give Aquamarine to Ahmad as a wife. Ahmad's first wife, a child bride, had died in childbirth months ago. She had been abducted from another village before Gaddo's arrival and in the camp had always worn a cheerful smile. It had been hard to tell if she was hurting or not. Now Ahmad wanted a more mature bride. Asmau was vehemently declaring that Aquamarine was older than sixteen, pointing out that they had been classmates in secondary school. But Aquamarine resisted, lying that she was only twelve.

Gaddo looked at Ahmad: she wouldn't wish an enemy to live under the same roof with that man. He was filthy. The edges of his heels were cracked and packed with dirt, as if he hadn't bathed in months. And he smelled like a goat.

"Aquamarine *is* twelve," said Gaddo, pushing herself into their circle. "It's true we were classmates and friends, but Aquamarine was double-promoted twice in her primary school because of her intelligence *fa*."

They all stared at Gaddo, and she stared right back.

"She doesn't even know what menstruation is," Gaddo said. "Or have you gotten your menses yet, Aquamarine?" She looked straight at her friend.

"No," Aquamarine said.

Asmau and Binta eyed the girls, and Malam Hamzah gave Aquamarine a mocking smile. He told her, "*Yaro*." Then he patted Ahmad on the shoulder and said, "Let's go. We will find you another bride."

Gaddo paused to stare at Asmau and Binta—first at one, then the other. Uneasy, the pair walked away, clearly disappointed and upset.

Now alone with Gaddo, Aquamarine thanked her for her quick thinking and then turned to hasten away, but Gaddo stopped her and asked how she was doing.

"Fine," Aquamarine answered, without looking at her friend. Her eyes were fixed on the road.

The last time they had spoken together was the day after Safiya's death. Aquamarine had been angry at Gaddo because her husband had taken part in the killing, though she knew Gaddo had no choice, that she was trapped in the union.

"I don't blame you," said Gaddo now. "I'll understand if you don't want to speak to me, if you believe I chose Kadir despite my

Christian upbringing and Safiya's murder to get away from the hardships of the camp. But there's something else." She was relieved to see Aquamarine's eyes shift in her direction.

"He's not as bad as he may seem. I—like him," said Gaddo. She was careful to use the word *like* instead of *love*, which was what she really felt for Kadir.

That had not always been true. When Malam Hamzah had first given her to Kadir as a wife, after she had converted to Islam, she had been upset that Kadir had specifically declared that she was his choice. She'd felt like a piece of *atampa* wrapper on a market stall table. But on their wedding night, when, instead of forcing himself on her, he had engaged her in talk, asking about her family, her life, her ambitions, her school, she began to realize how lucky she was, though she still didn't fully trust his intentions.

Gaddo could not share these shifting feelings with Aquamarine. She knew that whatever relationship the friends might rekindle now would be quenched if she dared to voice the truth.

"A killer is a killer," said Aquamarine.

"I know," Gaddo said. "But he's different. He is kind to me."

"I hope you know what you are doing," said Aquamarine. "And I hope you won't regret it. Good luck." She turned and walked away.

Gaddo felt truly alone then, abandoned. She wished she and Aquamarine could laugh and talk the way they used to at school. Instead, she was being judged for whom she loved.

Kadir returned that evening covered with dust. There were specks of dried blood on his cheeks and temples. But Gaddo didn't care if he had killed one hundred people or no one. She slipped out of her clothes and pulled him toward their mat. Then she unbuttoned his shirt and peeled it off. Kadir undid his belt and zipper and kicked off his trousers and boots. When Gaddo saw the size of his swollen manhood, her heart skipped; she had never before seen a naked man. Together they tumbled awkwardly onto the mat, then laughed at their awkwardness. As he lay on top of her, Gaddo marveled at the mixture of pain and pleasure, pain and pleasure that arose with Kadir's gentle thrusting.

Afterward, they lay in each other's arms, exhausted. Kadir's hot tears slid down Gaddo's shoulder.

"Let's leave," said Kadir. "Let's start our lives somewhere far away in the western part of the country."

These were the best words Gaddo had heard since arriving at the camp. She whispered, "I will go wherever you go." She pressed her cheek against Kadir's head.

Gaddo realized that, for the second time in two months, she had missed her monthly flow. She paced back and forth inside their hut, second-guessing herself, waiting for Kadir to return from a meeting with the other men.

But when Kadir returned, he had news. Finally there was a window for their escape. She would dress up in one of his uniforms, cover her face with a scarf, and join the men on their next raid in Kasar Lafiya. Then, during the mayhem, they would sneak away from the group. In town, they would change into civilian clothing, ease themselves into the community, then board a bus to Lagos or Ogun State. Kadir's savings would cover the costs of transportation and more. At worst, they could turn themselves into the military and say they had been captured against their will, which was the truth.

Gaddo told Kadir that his plan was perfect. Then she shared news of her pregnancy. She loved how he caught her cheeks in his hands and kissed her forehead.

She spent the remainder of the day fantasizing about freedom, about reuniting with her mother and other family members. Soon.

The next day, after Koran class, Gaddo waited, not far from the dadawa tree, for Aquamarine. She was exhausted: the class had been long and the heat was wretched. She doubted Aquamarine would want to speak to her after their last meeting, so she was surprised and glad when the girl walked up to her.

After greetings, Gaddo blurted out, "I think I'm pregnant. I've missed my period twice. That's not necessarily confirmation, but—."

"Well done." Aquamarine sighed.

"Meaning?"

"What else do you want me to say?" asked Aquamarine. "You married that killer. You should have known, sooner or later, you'd become pregnant with his child."

Gaddo stared at Aquamarine for a moment, choosing her next words carefully. "Where is the Aquamarine I knew? My friend, the encourager?"

"She died at the hostel," said Aquamarine. "Abduction? Remember? I hate being here."

In a low voice Gaddo said, "For an escape plan to work, a person might have to pretend to go along with things before she makes a move."

Aquamarine stared at Gaddo in disbelief.

Gaddo smiled at her friend's confusion. She wanted to say more, to tell her about her plan to escape with Kadir, but Asmau and Binta were walking past, pretending not to see them.

"I have to go," said Aquamarine. "Or else the other girls will eat all the lunch."

Gaddo reached out and hugged her friend. This might be their last chance to be alone, she thought. She shoved a large piece of buttered bread wrapped in black cellophane into Aquamarine's hand.

Aquamarine thanked her and hastened away.

Gaddo thought of Safiya, who was very zealous in her faith. She would never have accepted such a meal from her, not from a giver who had turned her back on Christianity and joined herself to a sinner bound for hellfire. Gaddo hoped Aquamarine would someday escape this camp and find her way home to her mother.

• • •

At the beginning of the next week, Malam Hamzah announced to his men that the raid on Kasar Lafiya had been postponed. He said that someone must have tipped off the military because the town had suddenly become fortified with troops. Nevertheless, Kadir told Gaddo that they would go on with their escape plan. Gaddo's pregnancy was already starting to show, and soon it might become difficult for her to fit into his uniform.

On Friday night that week, Gaddo and Kadir dressed themselves in Kadir's fake army uniforms and armed themselves with AK-47s. They succeeded in walking past all the camp watch posts without suspicion. But just before they entered the largely unoccupied parts of the forest, they met Malam Hamzah, Ahmad, and a few other men standing in a horizontal line.

"My Binta was right when she said she'd heard about an escape," said Malam Hamzah. "*Me yasa*, Kadir?—Why?"

Gaddo frowned and bowed her head. She could not meet Kadir's questioning gaze. She felt worthless, knowing that she had been responsible for accidentally tipping off Binta when she'd been speaking to Aquamarine. "Sorry. It was a mistake," she whispered to him. She wished she could strangle Binta for eavesdropping.

She was relieved to feel Kadir give her hand a reassuring squeeze. "I think the killings are senseless," said Kadir to Malam Hamzah. "We cause so many people so much hurt, so many losses, so much bloodshed."

"The infidel government asked for trouble when they killed our master years ago," said Malam Hamzah. "There will be no end to this war until we crush them and all they hold dear."

He asked them to return to the camp. But Gaddo pulled at Kadir's hand and said to Malam Hamzah, "Release us, please."

The glint in Malam Hamzah's eyes reminded her of his look on the day he'd ordered Safiya's stoning. Gaddo's heart lurched painfully in her chest, but she squared her shoulders and stared back at him. Safiya was Safiya. Gaddo is Gaddo. He should see the anger in her eyes, too.

She felt Kadir's grip tighten as Malam Hamzah closed the distance between them. But the man just gave Kadir a friendly pat on the shoulder and suggested that they talk over the matter like adults back at the camp.

Kadir nodded quietly. "We will walk."

Back to the camp? Gaddo wanted to grumble to Kadir, but the words died on her tongue when she saw the wild fear in his eyes as he turned and looked at her. Many thoughts scrambled into her mind. She remembered that he had said that Malam Hamzah and his people would hunt down any deserters. What might they face when they reached the camp? She hoped Kadir would convince Malam Hamzah to pardon them—to this point, he had been one of Malam Hamzah's favored fighters.

Gaddo and Kadir walked hand in hand. When they were out of hearing distance, he said, "I did not make a fuss because they would have easily gunned us down. But tomorrow is another day to plot, if we live to see tomorrow."

Gaddo nodded and squeezed his hand. "Tomorrow is another day."

At the camp, armed men ordered Gaddo to remain inside their hut and took Kadir away. The night was cold without him at her side. She tossed and turned on the mat. She was hopeful that he might squeeze out a pardon from Malam Hamzah, but she wondered why their discussion was taking so long. She fell asleep and then was jolted awake a few minutes after midnight by the distant crack of a gun. She had a sudden uneasy feeling and began to worry about Kadir's whereabouts. She was determined to stay awake until he returned, but exhaustion overcame her and she soon fell into a slumber.

At 6 a.m. there was a sharp knock on her door. When she opened it, she was greeted by Kadir's corpse on a pallet, a large bullet hole in his forehead. That forehead where she used to read his pain and confusion, during all those nights that they'd shared on their mat. She remembered her dream of Kadir lying lifeless inside a coffin, only there had been no bullet hole in his forehead. She remembered that he had asked her to talk about the dream, but she had refused and then had forgotten about it. Had fate given her that dream to warn him? Had she failed him? She screamed his name, fell on his corpse, began to shake his body.

Ahmad, who had led the pallbearers to Gaddo's door, gripped her arms and pulled her away from the corpse. He said, "It's a stupid man who will take a shot for his woman. When I pulled the trigger, I made sure he felt like the pig that he was."

Without warning, Gaddo turned and jumped on Ahmad, catching his left ear with her teeth. Ahmad squealed in pain and punched at her midriff. The other men tried to yank Gaddo away, but she wound her arms around Ahmad's neck and tore at his earlobe. A crowd of girls had gathered, some girls calling her name, others—among them, Aquamarine—cursing the men for handling her roughly.

Finally, Gaddo finally let go of Ahmad. She spat a piece of his ear onto the ground and wiped blood off her mouth with the back of her hand.

Ahmad cursed and lurched at her, but the other men held him back. Then a searing pain shot through the center of Gaddo's being. She felt as if everything inside her body—her brain, her lungs, her bowels—was being sucked out from between her legs. Aquamarine and a few other girls ran from the crowd and caught Gaddo's hands to keep her from crashing to the ground.

"She's bleeding," said Aquamarine. "We have to help her."

With his hand over his torn ear, Ahmad said to Gaddo, "You are mine now, never forget."

Those were the last words she heard before she fainted.

AQUAMARINE

Aquamarine and about sixty other girls, some of them not from her school, sat beneath the giant dadawa tree and listened to Malam Rafik, the Koran class tutor, preach from the Hadith of love.

She felt faint from the heat of the May sun, but not so faint as to give in when Malam Rafik began to sweet-talk the girls into converting from their Christian faith.

"If you do," he urged, "you will be married to one of our men, who will take good care of you, and you will be moved from this open space to more comfortable dwellings."

Aquamarine and the girls laughed at him. *He must think that we are fools like the other girls who've decided to bind themselves to brutes*, she thought.

"Why don't you follow the example of your classmates and friends?" said Malam Rafik. "They usually have extra to eat."

"We will not change our religion," shouted Jemimah.

Quickly, other girls joined in, repeating her shout, trying to drown out the skinny man's voice.

"We are married to Jesus," some cried.

"This tree is okay for us," others squealed.

"Take us back home to our families," Aquamarine hollered, and Malam Rafik turned and fixed her with a stare.

"This will remain your home if you do not do as I say," said Malam Rafik. "And I mean all of you."

The girls all fell silent and watched the tutor walk away. But he hadn't taken more than four steps when the first bomb dropped from the sky, landing about eighty meters away from the tree, raising a plume of sand, hurling scraps of wood and metal into the air. The girls huddled at the foot of the dadawa tree for safety. Then another bomb dropped, this time even closer, and some of the girls began scampering haphazardly from tree to tree, not knowing where the next bomb might drop.

The bombs fell faster and faster as the men in the camp fired back. Panting with fear, Aquamarine lay flat on the vibrating ground, her palms plastered over her ears. Beneath her body she felt lumps of stony sand and knotweeds. Her nostrils filled with the odor of plowed earth mixed with the bombs' rotten-egg stink. Had the military forgotten that the girls they wanted to rescue lived among the terrorists they sought to destroy? She moved her lips silently in prayer.

After what seemed like an hour, the shooting stopped and the fighter jets vanished from the sky. Malam Hamzah and his men began to count their losses. Scores of men had been killed, many wounded, and five girls were dead. Jemimah was one of them.

That night, as Aquamarine lay on the ground beneath the dadawa tree, her old day wear serving as her mat, she watched the dark clouds drifting across the sky. Some blocked the new moon momentarily from her view, then drifted away, leaving the moon shining faintly. Aquamarine thought how close she had come to dying Kubra's kind of death—to being blown into smithereens. She resolved to find her way home, soon, by any means possible.

Three days later, after the midday Koran class, Malam Hamzah arrived at the dadawa tree and stood before the girls.

"We need girls who want to go to heaven," he said. "Who would like to wear a vest and go to paradise?"

The girls looked from one to the other in amazement. Some found the statement funny. Others were upset.

How rich an offer, Aquamarine sneered to herself. She knew that putting on a suicide vest, stepping outside this camp into free society, just meant blowing oneself up.

"Some of the girls who escaped from this and other camps have been talking to journalists," Malam Hamzah said. "Now the attacks against us have multiplied and become concentrated. Someone even tipped off the army of that rogue country of infidels, told them of our whereabouts. So we must send them a message, teach them not to bother us in our caliphate."

Aquamarine thought his words made no sense. When had this forest stopped being part of Nigeria?

"We will send them little gifts," Malam Hamzah said. He smiled and turned his gaze to Aquamarine and the other tiny girls in the group. He gestured, and some of his men stepped forward with black vests. He took one into his hand and stooped before a little girl, a child of ten, and asked, "Would you like to wear a vest and go to town? To the market? To church? I will give you plenty of sweets."

That girl stared blankly at him, but a few of the very little girls said they would like to put on a vest and get sweets. Shocked, Aquamarine stared at Malam Hamzah. How could he take advantage of their ignorance and innocence? She wanted to shout at him to put on one of those vests and go do the job himself, but then a new version of his words played in her head: *wear a vest, get sweets, go to town, escape the camp.* Was this her chance?

Aquamarine's hand shot up. "I will wear a vest and get some sweets."

Malam Hamzah looked in her direction and nodded. A few more girls agreed to wear vests, and Aquamarine worried that her private escape agenda was now encouraging other girls to go on suicide missions that would kill unsuspecting innocents at home.

Malam Hamzah congratulated the vest volunteers and made big promises to them. Then some of his men herded the volunteers to their new lodging, a big hut not far from the dadawa tree.

Since arriving at the camp in April of last year, Aquamarine had never been offered as much food as she was given on the vest wearers' first night in their new hut. Some of the girls began to believe that they had made an excellent decision. And though Aquamarine was focused on the hope of escape, she was glad she could sleep without worrying about scorpions or army ants or snakes, all of which had plagued the girls who had sheltered, in rain and shine, beneath the dadawa tree.

Holding a steaming plate of *shinkafa*, dotted with orange tomato stew and shreds of smoked fish, Aquamarine remembered the chickens that Auntie Ijeoma had kept in her backyard. She remembered how her auntie would order her to feed the chickens extra well during the few weeks before Christmas, to fatten them for holiday tables. Now, though Aquamarine felt like one of Auntie Ijeoma's chickens, she wolfed down her food, wiped her plate with her fingers, and licked them. Meanwhile, she listened to Abdulmalik, the commandant in charge of suicide explosions.

Abdulmalik passed out Tom-Tom candies, and the girls were happy to be tasting bits of home once again. Then he mentioned that the vests would be loaded with explosives, and their mood changed. As they began to protest, he quickly added that the girls would be taken to a big house with water flowing from its taps. There would be lots of treats. The girls settled down and listened once more. Aquamarine was surprised that some still hadn't fully caught on to what would happen to them.

Abdulmalik then emphasized that only those who were devout members of the caliphate would be allowed to put on the vests and go to the big house in town. If they were sworn to the holy mission, then they would go straight to heaven after killing the infidels of the rogue country.

"You have to recite the Shahada," he said.

Aquamarine believed that she could avoid blowing herself up; that had been her plan all along. But she didn't want to give up her Catholic faith. She would rather opt out of the mission. Renouncing her faith would make her a sellout, like Gaddo, who, after Kadir's death, had been forcibly taken to another camp by Ahmad as his wife. Perhaps she could lie, say that she had a migraine or feign asthma. But then an idea popped into her mind. She could pretend to be a devout convert, go through the training, and then refuse to detonate the bomb. She smiled at her genius, peeled the wrapper off the candy, and tucked the sweet into her mouth. Suddenly she thought, *What if they set a timer on the vest bomb?* She felt like spitting out the Tom-Tom.

Next morning, the girls lined up in a clearing in the forest, watching and listening intently as Abdulmalik explained how to work a suicide vest: everything from putting it on to detonating it. A little girl, about nine years old, asked, "Will we see our mama and baba in heaven when we explode?"

Abdulmalik nodded. "But only if your mama and baba follow your example and hold on to the holy faith. We will make sure they come and meet you soon in heaven."

Aquamarine wished she could wash Abdulmalik's words out of the girl's brain.

After answering a few more questions, Abdulmalik told the girls they would receive training for two more days before being sent on their individual assignments.

After that day's training, Aquamarine walked past the dadawa tree to her new lodging. She knew that the girls with whom she had once lived were eying her as she walked past. She was sure she heard someone whisper, "Shameless traitor." She hurried on, not looking in their direction. Now she understood how Gaddo must have felt when she'd judged her for marrying Kadir. Aquamarine wished she could tell the girls that her investment in the mission was simply a plot for escape. She would die before she abandoned her faith.

At the door of the hut, Binta and a heavily pregnant Asmau accosted her. "They are looking for girls younger than twelve to wear the vests," said Asmau. "You and I know very well that you are older."

"I'm twelve," Aquamarine said. "Remember, I was double-promoted twice in my primary school." She marveled at how smoothly Gaddo's lie flowed from her mouth. And she felt thankful for her friend and wished they were together.

"You're not a devout Muslim," said Binta.

Aquamarine leaned forward and rattled off the Shahada with gusto. She liked their open-mouthed stares, how they looked at each other in surprise and backed away.

Entering the hut, she shut the door after herself and caught sight of eleven-year-old Sara sitting in the corner and chanting to herself, "I can do this. I can do this." Other than the two of them, the room was empty.

Aquamarine had always marveled at Sara's lovely oval face, which reminded her of Kubra's. Grace's nickname for Kubra had been "Chocolate Beauty." But there were differences: Sara was more than a head shorter than Kubra, and Kubra had had a broken tooth and a small scar above her left eyebrow, the result of a fall during track practice in ninth grade.

Sara and another girl had been assigned to bomb the Gwagwalala market, and the mission would take place the following day. Aquamarine sat at the other end of the room and imagined the customers she had seen at the market. She wished she could stop the bombing.

After a few more rounds of chanting, Sara stopped and turned toward Aquamarine. "I'm doing this to calm my nerves."

Aquamarine nodded to Sara. "Why do you want to wear a vest?"

"I don't know," said Sara. "Perhaps, because the men said we should, and God would be happy with us."

Aquamarine stayed silent, feeling great distress. Adults were meant to protect little children, not brainwash them and lead them to destruction in the name of God.

"Do you get scared?" asked Sara.

"I'm afraid of blowing up my friends and the parents who love me," said Aquamarine. Even as she spoke, she knew that *love* was not the word to describe the parents who had given her away, especially her father. Yet she hoped that Sara would imagine her own loving parents and think twice about continuing the mission.

"But then we will all go to heaven as Abdulmalik said," said Sara.

"I think we need to do good deeds to enter heaven," Aquamarine responded.

"Like wearing a vest for God as Abdulmalik said," Sara said.

Aquamarine hoped karma would punish Abdulmalik for packing the girl's head with his stupid sayings. She wished she could tell Sara her real thoughts about suicide bombing and about Abdulmalik, but she assumed that Sara would repeat them—*Aquamarine said this, Aquamarine said that*—and she would get into trouble. So she kept silent and tried to force herself to take a siesta. But sleep refused to come. She imagined herself exploding. She imagined how Kubra might have felt just before she exploded. She imagined whether going through with the bombing wouldn't just make life easy, no more troubles with terrorists, no more suffering and pain in the camp. She drifted off to sleep, woke, drifted again, and in one of her wakeful moments saw Kubra standing by the entrance door with a mournful look in her eyes. There was no mistaking that oval face and the small scar above the left eyebrow. Aquamarine felt dizzy.

"Kubra," she said. In a flash, the image vanished. Aquamarine looked around to be sure it wasn't Sara at the door. But Sara was sound asleep. A caution? Aquamarine thought. Then she, too, fell asleep.

Three days later, Abdulmalik told the girls that Sara and her partner had successfully blown up the Gwagwalala market and had killed sixteen infidels, wounding many more. Aquamarine hoped that Sergeant, that familiar face, that comforter in her sadness, in those days when her anger at her auntie was so strong, was not among them. She felt sad that Sara had died. Abdulmalik then announced the names of the girls who would take part in the next mission. Aquamarine was one of them. She was assigned to blow up the IDP camp on the outskirts of Kasar Lafiya and Dabu, the neighboring town. Wretchedly unhappy, Aquamarine hardly spoke to anyone as the mission day approached.

She had terrible nightmares, such bad ones that she began to fear that her escape plan would fall through. The night before the mission, she barely slept at all. So many thoughts milled inside her head. She thought about the gossip in school about a neighbor who'd seen a vulture fly away with a chunk of Kubra. She thought about Safiya's preaching about mansions in heaven. She thought about Grace and wondered if she'd found her way home. She thought about her mother and wondered how she would react to learning that her daughter was a suicide bomber.

When she finally fell asleep, she found herself standing on a riverbank and looking out into the water. Suddenly, the water transformed into a multitude of people, all pointing accusing fingers at her. She fled, and they chased her. The road she ran down was never-ending, and the people wouldn't stop chasing her.

Aquamarine jerked awake, panting and soaked in sweat. It was 4 a.m. and Abdulmalik was banging on the door of their hut, shouting that it was time to go.

Once the two girls were outside, Abdulmalik blindfolded them. They walked for a few meters and were then hoisted onto a truck that drove for hours. The air was suffocating, and sweat plastered Aquamarine's niqab to her skin.

When the truck finally halted, Aquamarine was lifted down. She was relieved to be on solid ground once again. Someone pulled off her blindfold. She squinted and found herself in the company of two kaftan-clad strangers in an open field. The other girl was still blindfolded, still in the back of the covered truck, guarded by two men also dressed in kaftans. As the truck roared away, the men strapped the suicide vest to Aquamarine's torso under her niqab.

Then, with a red marker, one drew a zigzag map on Aquamarine's palm, indicating the turns she should take to get to the IDP camp. He insisted that if anyone were to stop her and ask questions, she should simply say she lived in the camp.

Aquamarine nodded.

"We are right behind you," the man said. "Do not fail. God's arms are wide open to receive you in paradise. God is the greatest!"

Aquamarine nodded. "God is the greatest," she repeated.

"If you do not have the courage to tug on the wire, we have made plans to help you," said the man. "We have fixed two sets of explosives. One, you can control. The other, we control." The man showed her a black handset.

Wide-eyed, Aquamarine nodded. She hadn't seen this coming. If she decided not to detonate the bomb, the men would "help" her. So how would she escape? "God is the greatest," she said again. Maybe if she showed enough confidence, the men wouldn't try to get involved.

They nodded at her and Aquamarine walked away.

Taking the first turn on her map, Aquamarine found herself in front of the Monday market. The men had disappeared into the crowd, but she could still feel their eyes following her every move. Maybe there were many more eyes following her. She looked at her palm, took the next turn, and soon found herself in the quarter that housed the Fulfulde IDP camp. Her heart began to thump as each step drew her closer to the dilapidated gates. There was no fence around the camp, only a guard hut occupied by two police officers who wore military scarves as shields against the dust. Large sandbags were piled in front of the hut, protection from potential attackers. There was a large black drum beside the barricade, perhaps where they lit watch fires at night.

In front of the entrance a couple of men were mixing concrete, getting ready to repair a broken section of the gates. Women were busy with various activities—washing clothes, feeding babies, sewing, knitting, chatting, laughing, cooking. The camp's ramshackle houses, all made of aluminum sheathing, were tightly packed into rows. Aquamarine imagined how hot those houses must be, with the sun battering down on them. She saw a faded blue water tank perched on a spidery metal platform. A group of children, just released from class, ran out to join other children in a distant red-mud field; she could see that they were playing soccer with a torn multicolored ball. Other children raced toward the living quarters. *How can I waste all of these lives?* she thought.

Just as Aquamarine reached the gates, the policemen stopped her and asked her if she lived in the camp.

Aquamarine looked over her shoulder to check if the kaftan-clad men had followed her. She didn't see them but had a strong feeling that there was a remote control out there waiting to blow her apart if she failed.

"Yes, and I need to use the bathroom right away," she said, waving her hands wildly.

The policemen laughed. "We still have to search you," said the darker-skinned one.

Now Aquamarine raised her arms in surrender. She said, "I have a bomb."

The policemen jumped to their feet, snatched out their guns, took cover. Aquamarine stood like a statue, staring into the barrels.

The men mixing concrete fled.

"Do you want me to remove the bomb?" bellowed the darker-skinned policemen.

"Yes," said Aquamarine.

"It's a setup!" shouted the other policeman, trigger cocked. "Officer-in-charge, na wahala this girl carry come here."

Aquamarine saw that his partner was losing faith in her. She said, "Help me, please. Some men have the remote control, and they are watching me. If you try to remove the bomb here, they will punch the button."

"Take off your niqab," said the darker-skinned policeman.

"You no fit trust these children," said the other policeman. "Most are brainwashed."

Aquamarine began to unwrap the black cloth on her head, but the darker-skinned policeman suddenly ordered her to stop. He told her to walk to the water tank and wait.

She followed his instructions, as both policemen watched warily. In a moment, the two men stepped forward and carefully helped take off her niqab. Then the darker-skinned man cut off the vest with a pair of scissors and defused the bomb.

Instantly, Aquamarine knelt and thanked them, pouring blessings on them and their families.

The darker-skinned man pulled her to her feet, then rolled down his scarf. When Aquamarine saw the tribal scarifications on his face, she cried, "Sergeant!"

"My color," Sergeant said.

He asked Aquamarine to describe the men who had brought her in the truck. But her descriptions didn't help much, given that most local men had beards and wore kaftans.

Still, Sergeant said to his colleague, "Vigilance and protocol will make a difference. Search whoever must be searched, and shine our eyes well-well."

As Sergeant led her to the living quarters of the camp, Aquamarine told him about her experiences. He listened quietly, but she knew he was sorry. After she told him that his efforts to cheer her up at the Gwagwalala market had been light in her darkness, he told her about growing up in Warri, about losing his daughter during the Niger Delta militancy crisis, about his resolve to always share joy with everyone.

They stopped at the entrance of the largest shack, and Sergeant called out to Kaka, an elderly woman who was in charge of the camp's women and children, and placed Aquamarine in her care. Aquamarine spent that night in one of the block structures deep inside the camp. She slept on a thin mattress on the floor. The last time she had slept on a mattress had been on the day of her abduction, which now seemed like ages ago.

When morning came, Aquamarine noticed a blackboard in the room, with quadratic equations written in white chalk. She smiled and breathed the word "School." She remembered the moment when the two men had strapped her with the vest. She had been afraid to breathe, in case the rise and fall of her chest would cause the bomb to detonate automatically. When she'd discovered that she wouldn't blow up when she breathed, she'd felt a kind of release.

Now with the terror of the camp behind her, she felt a stronger kind of release. Still lying on the mattress, she stretched her limbs, delighting in her newfound freedom. She imagined herself on a bus headed for Enugu and then immediately felt another cage creep around her heart—the fear of facing her mother.

Kaka greeted Aquamarine with a bowl of *jollof* rice and a large piece of fried beef. Aquamarine sat for a few minutes without eating, staring at the food. Now that she had escaped, everything felt surreal, including the fact of having such a lovely meal all to herself. Eventually she ate, and as she did she asked Kaka what life in the IDP camp was like.

"The government, NGOs and well-meaning Nigerians are trying to help, with donations and supplies and a lot more," she said. "But after a while, you really want to go back home because there is no place like home."

Aquamarine nodded, asking Kaka where her home was and why she was in the camp.

"The Baga massacre," said Kaka. "Corpses everywhere. I fled with my five children after my husband was beheaded in our presence. Some scenes remain stamped on the memory forever, but life goes on, and so must I."

"My warmest sympathy for your loss," said Aquamarine.

The next morning, Sergeant drove Aquamarine to the motor park on his motorcycle. He told her he that had called for more police presence at the camp, and he offered to pay her bus fare to Enugu since her abductors had stripped her of everything valuable. Somehow, though, she had managed to hide the piece of paper with her father's phone number. She would arrive in Enugu on the following afternoon, so she would have time to locate her family before nightfall. Aquamarine was grateful for Sergeant's help, grateful also that he waited until she had safely boarded and the bus had belched into the road, heading south.

"Enugu, here I come," Aquamarine said to herself and relaxed into her seat.

GRACE

Giving the brown-bean porridge one last stir, Grace turned off the stove and spooned the beans onto the plates that her brothers, Daniel and Luke, held out to her. She then filled plates for her father and herself and carried them to the dining table. Each person said their own blessings, silently.

Then Daniel ate a spoonful and immediately chewed on a stone. Spitting it into his palm, he held it up like a prized possession and said in a mock wistful tone, “Hmm, if stones were diamonds, I’d be richer than that person who plots to destroy my teeth by putting stones into her beanpot.”

Luke laughed. Grace smiled.

“Perhaps,” said their father. “If you or Luke had helped Grace pick stones out of the beans while she was pounding pepper and chopping onions, no one would have chewed on one.”

He put a spoonful into his own mouth and instantly bit a stone. Everyone burst into laughter.

“Sorry, Baba,” said Grace. “Next time I’ll make sure they pound the pepper and chop the onions so I can have the time to pick out the stones.”

"Very good," her father said.

"Nooo," the brothers chorused, contorting their faces to show their disapproval.

"When Helen cooked, there never used to be stones in the rice or beans," said Daniel.

"And she never made us pound pepper or cut onions," added Luke.

"That was because Grace was there to help her most of the time, except when she was at school," said their father.

At the mention of Helen, Grace saddened. She remembered Helen's last phone call, on the day before the school was attacked by terrorists. She remembered her father's futile search for Helen at Gujba and Damaturu in the months following Helen's disappearance. She didn't want to imagine that Helen was dead. She also didn't want to imagine that she had been captured and was wasting away in some terrorist camp. Grace wondered what had become of her friends—Aquamarine, Gaddo, and Safiya. She hoped they were safe. She would never forget the sight and sound of those gigantic trucks roaring away into the night, filled with her friends and classmates as she, an escapee, peeked from her hiding place in the bushes.

After jumping from the moving truck, Grace had huddled in the bushes until daybreak, hoping to meet up with Aquamarine. She never found her friend, but she did encounter a few other girls who had escaped. Ntala was one of them, and together they'd trekked through the forest back to their school and then found their various ways home.

Two weeks later, Grace was scrolling through the contacts in her phone, looking for a number saved as *Aquamarine's runaway father.* Finding it, she paused, sighed, then pressed the back key and set her phone aside. She was longing to know if Aquamarine had succeeded in jumping off the trailer, if she had made her way home to Enugu. She had already visited Aquamarine's auntie in the new residential area of the town, hoping to discover what the family was doing about Aquamarine's abduction. But the woman no longer lived there. To this point, Grace had not had the courage to call Aquamarine's father.

How would she respond if he asked questions about her friend that she didn't have answers to? Every time she made up her mind to call him, she would put her phone down again.

Now, at the table, Grace asked her father about his vigilante job, the community security group made up of local hunters who supported the military in fending off terrorists. Her father replied that the government was promising to send more troops to the town because the terrorists had regained some of the ground they had lost to the military.

"Baba," said Daniel. "I want to go to work with you tonight."

"Me, too," said Luke.

"Baba, don't listen to them," Grace begged. "After eating so much bean porridge, they'll just fall asleep on the job and snore loud enough for all of Kasar Lafiya to hear."

The family laughed.

The boys frequently asked to go out with the vigilantes, but each time they did Grace invented another flimsy excuse to convince their father to leave them at home. Her comical explanations masked her fear for their safety, her desire to shield them from the unknown. Since her abduction ordeal, she had become extra-protective of everyone dear to her heart. Her father had received paramilitary training for the job, so he could defend himself. But what about her brothers? They had never received such training.

"Last Friday was night vigil in church," said Luke. "I stayed awake till dawn, so I know I can stay awake with you."

"But vigilante work is different from night vigil," explained their father. "People die on duty. It is not for children. Let's hope our new president's promise to end terrorism in Nigeria will come true."

He scraped up the last bits of porridge on his plate, and Grace offered to fetch him more. Yes, he said, but only if there was enough for everyone to have seconds. Grace assured him she had made plenty: she had cooked two extra *mudus* because, an hour after eating, the boys were always hungry again.

"We need the extra food. We're growing," said Daniel. At fourteen, his shoulders were already as broad as their father's, and his arms were just as long. Twelve-year-old Luke, with his lanky legs, showed every sign of following suit.

"Growing boys," he said and flexed his lean muscles.

There was a knock on the door, and Daniel offered to answer it. Their father's friend, Uncle Jomo, usually visited in the evening. The two men would sit and play cards or watch the news or football until 11 p.m., when they would leave for their vigilante shifts. As Daniel moved toward the door, Grace slipped into the kitchen, preparing to fill her father's plate and offer a serving to Uncle Jomo.

But just as she slapped out a spoonful of beans onto a side plate, she heard strange harsh voices and the sound of crushing metal. Quietly she dropped the spoon, tip-toed to the cracked-open kitchen door, and peeped out. Five armed men were pointing rifles at her father, her brothers, and Uncle Jomo. Blood streamed from a gash on her father's temple. The left side of his white cotton shirt was red and soaked with blood. The men must have forced Uncle Jomo to lead them to her father.

As Grace yanked her phone from her skirt pocket and punched in the police emergency number, the man in front of her father said, "Mr. Addoh, you led the vigilante group that killed one of our young men. You take one, we take two."

Without warning, two other men fired point-blank at Daniel and Luke. The boys slumped to the floor. Blood zig-zagged down the wall behind them.

Something exploded inside Grace's head. She wanted to scream, but grasped her throat instead, trying to smother the impulse. Why was there no answer from the police? Now her father suddenly ducked, kicked the speaker in the groin, snatched his rifle, but instantly three other men were on top of him, taking away the rifle, forcing him onto his knees. One struck him on the side of his head, and blood began to pour from the wound. All of the rifles were now trained on her father, except for the one muzzle pressed to Uncle Jomo's temple.

"We heard you have a daughter," said the man her father had kicked. "Where is she?"

"Away," he said.

"There are four plates on the table," said another man. "She must be somewhere."

Grace looked down at her phone and realized that she hadn't pressed the send button. Yanking open the back door, she ran into the night, running and running. She heard shots behind her. She knew what she would find when she came back to the house with the police.

The burials took place a week later, organized by Pastor Benjamin, who oversaw the Pentecostal church that Grace and her family usually attended. On July 1, the day after the funerals, Grace fell into a catatonic state. The only words she spoke were monosyllables: "Yes." "No." Sometimes her tongue wouldn't move at all.

Pastor Benjamin had already taken Grace into his home, and now he and his wife, Deaconess Kemi, focused on caring for her. They prayed and fasted for her recovery, brought in physical therapists, medical doctors, trauma specialists, psychiatrists, and prayer warriors, yet for two months her condition remained unchanged. The doctors could find no damage to her neurosystem. She wasn't suffering from a disease or an illness. The medical reports all stated that she was in perfect health. Perhaps, thought her caregivers, time would work its healing power.

Early on, Grace had tried to move her arms and her legs, but the limbs simply refused to budge. So she gave up trying. Everything seemed pointless. Why should she hope to find her father alive in their sitting room, to watch her brothers rise from the dead, arguing about everything under the sun? Why should she hope that Helen would walk through the door?

She felt grateful to Pastor Benjamin and Deaconess Kemi for their help, but she didn't know how to respond to their kindness. She felt she didn't deserve it; this must be why she had suffered so many losses. She even felt irritated by their kindness, telling herself that it would surely end soon, never allowing herself to get used to it. She couldn't bring herself to thank anyone or show any form of appreciation.

Life went on this way for weeks. Then, in mid-October, the church began preparations for its upcoming Christmas concert. Members of the choir compiled a list of twenty-five song suggestions, with the goal of reducing the list to fifteen. During one meeting an argument arose when someone suggested that they should include the Latin version of "Veni, Veni, Emmanuel."

During the argument Grace lay awake on her bed, counting the squares on the white ceiling of her room. Her window overlooked the church auditorium as well as the hall where the choir practiced. Since July, Grace had heard many things through her open window—some amusing, some disturbing, some embarrassing. She had heard gossip about church members, pastors, and church politics. She had heard prayers, expressions of gratitude, weeping, laughter, scolding, marriage proposals, rejection of marriage proposals, acceptance of marriage proposals, singing, preaching, disagreements.

Now she stopped her counting and tuned her ears to the argument about the song.

Someone said, "We are Pentecostal, not Anglican or Catholic. That song has orthodox influences."

Another said, "Have you ever heard people singing Kirk Franklin's or Pernam Percy Paul's songs in any Catholic church?"

"*Haba*," said another voice. "People praise God in different languages and tongues and God accepts them all. What makes a song of praise to God any different? Regardless of who wrote it or who sings it, God will still accept it if it is sung in his honor."

That seemed to settle the argument because Grace heard them begin to practice "Veni, Veni, Emmanuel." Grace knew she had heard the song before. Aquamarine had hummed herself to sleep with it on the day she'd received that letter of rejection from her mother. Then, the song had struck Grace as sad, perhaps because she knew Aquamarine was hurting. But today, as she lay in her bed, listening over and over to the song, it seemed to enter her heart, become part of her yearning to be free of pain. She stood up and opened the window wide so she could hear the lyrics and the deep soulfulness of the voices, which, to her, sounded almost like anguished wails.

Veni, veni, O Oriens,
Solare nos adveniens . . .

Grace wished one of the choir members would read the translation aloud. Though the song was beautiful, it was also haunting in a pleasant way, and she wanted to know what it meant. Even when the choir had moved on to other songs, Grace stood at the window, gazing at the sky, humming "Veni, Veni, Emmanuel."

A knock at the door startled her. She was even more startled when Deaconess Kemi walked into the room and screamed, "Miracle!" Only then did Grace remember her months of frozen stillness.

The scream brought Pastor Benjamin rushing into the room. When he saw Grace standing by the window, he knelt, threw his hands in the air, and began speaking in tongues. Deaconess Kemi, too, dropped to her knees and started speaking this unintelligible language. For ten minutes they spoke these strange words, and Grace stayed by the window, watching the choir members disperse after practice. They had no idea that their singing had helped her recover. Now, hearing the voices behind her die away, she turned and looked at Pastor Benjamin and Deaconess Kemi. They, too, were unaware of her gratitude. No one would know if she didn't tell them.

"Thank you for your kindness," Grace said.

The pair nodded and sighed, which she knew meant that they were glad that the forces that had held her captive had finally released her. Then they told her about an American missionary couple who had recently attended a pastors' conference in Lagos. At the meeting Pastor Benjamin had told the tale of Grace's ordeal and described the challenges of terrorism in the northern regions of Nigeria. The missionaries were in the house, and now they wanted to meet her.

In the sitting room, Grace shook hands with Bill and Meaghan McCleary, a middle-aged white couple who said they'd had the call of God to adopt orphans from around the world and in the United States. Their palms felt oddly soft. The two told her about their adopted son, Jake, and daughter, Amal, a Syrian Christian orphaned in the Syrian crisis, and invited her to join the family in Florida, all expenses paid, if she cared to go.

"Florida." Grace smiled dryly. She and her siblings used to argue about the best tourist attractions in America, comparing them to Nigeria's. She had always wanted to visit Disney World in Florida. But she had never imagined that, when the opportunity came, no one in her family would be alive to share the moment with her.

Nonetheless, Grace nodded her acceptance. Though she was thankful for the offer, there was no excitement in her heart. Even as the adults in the room cheered for her, all she could see in their smiles were the faces of her father, her brothers, her mother (who had died while birthing Luke), and Helen. A lump formed in her chest.

KUBRA'S HEAVEN

A week before the third Christmas after my death, I hovered over the scene of my accident. The harmattan had made the midday sun hazy. I noticed that the pothole created by the car explosion had widened and was now a huge crater. Drivers swerved away from the spot, which after days of rain had become a broad murky pool. The bungalow, the one I'd seen draped with parts of my flesh, had long since been torn down, and a dirty brown duplex occupied its spot. Along the street, herdsmen slung with AK-47s drove cattle that gobbled up every inch of greenery along their path, dropping heaps of dung as they passed.

Whitish harmattan dust clouded the windows of our house. Though the little patch of grass beside the walkway was yellow and parched from the dry wind, the place had an air of calm. Mother and Danladi were certainly at home. In Christmases past, Mother would usually prepare bottles of *zoborodo* and crunchy *kuli-kuli* for the visitors who would come by after Christmas church service and on New Year's Day. I used to help with the preparations and would munch up a good portion of the freshly fried *kuli-kuli*, much to her irritation. "*Wannan 'yata tana son kuli-kuli da yawa,*" she would say, shaking her head at me for liking *kuli-kuli* too much, especially since I disliked fruit a lot, and then she would warn Danladi not to follow my example. Otherwise, she said, *kuli-kuli* would grow like brush inside his stomach. I remembered that, on Christmas of 2015, Mother had prepared fewer bottles of *zoborodo,* fewer trays of *kuli-kuli.* I remembered watching her chew a piping hot stick of *kuli-kuli,* blowing steam out of her mouth as she tried to cool her tongue. When she offered some to Danladi, he refused, saying, "Hot-hot. No bush inside my stomach." Mother laughed, giving him a you-will-soon-grow-out-of-my-white-lies look, and muttered to herself, "Kubra must have had a freezer in her mouth."

In front of Mama Lakhmi's ugly house, I noticed a few unhealthy-looking hibiscus shrubs, their shriveled red flowers coated with harmattan dust. She didn't visit Mother so often these days, not since their disagreement about Mother's decision to take a new job. At the start of the new academic session in September, with renovations going on at the burned-down school and classes taking place in makeshift tents, the principal had been sacked for making decisions that had led to the student abductions. Mother had been offered the open position, but Mama-Lakhmi had tried to discourage her from accepting it, which upset Mother and made her question their friendship. Mother took the job as acting principal.

Malam Balarabe's kiosk had grown more robust since my death. He now sold many more provisions as well as toys such as plastic footballs and colorful monster and Santa masks that were popular with children.

As I was watching, Danladi peeked out of one of our windows, then vanished from sight. I knew he must be engrossed in play, and I drifted over to see what he was up to. I was still amazed at how easily I could pass through concrete walls. Such moments gave me pleasure, though at other times I bewailed my untimely passing, furious at why I hadn't found the key to my home in heaven. At these times my body would briefly disintegrate, just as it had done during the explosion. But when my rage cooled, my head, my shoulders, my hands, my flanks, my legs would reunite into this pervious form.

Now that I was in the house, I could see that one of Malam Balarabe's Santa masks was dangling from Danladi's neck. The elastic band had stretched out, and he was in Mother's room, rummaging through her trinket basket, probably searching for bobby pins to hold it in place. I watched him rifle through the pins but then stop and pick up an envelope from the basket. He opened the envelope, looked inside, stared down at five charred teeth.

Mother came into the room at that moment, ready to ask if Danladi had found the pins. Then he turned and she saw the envelope in his hands. She hastened forward, took it from him, folded down the flap, and tucked it back into the basket. She picked out two bobby pins and handed them to him.

"Mami, we know what happened to Kubra," Danladi said. "But when is Father coming home?"

Mother sighed. "My dear, I have no idea. I don't understand how your father just disappeared from the face of the earth, *gaskiya*. There is no trace of the bus he entered, no record of him in any accident, and no corpses anywhere, whether on land or sea. Only heaven knows."

Danladi pinned on the mask. The white-rimmed cutouts made his eyes seem huge and twinkly.

Mother took his hand and led him toward the sitting room. "Let us just assume that an angel took your father on loan."

Mother rambled on. But Danladi's mouth was set in a pout, and I knew he was frowning under his mask. It was a familiar expression, one that my brother wore when he struggled to understand an instruction or a statement.

I, too, had always wondered why Father had traveled west and never returned. Aquamarine's father had done the same, and this shared experience—being the daughters of "The Runaway Fathers"—had helped us form a tight bond.

• • •

Months ago, in October, I had tried to explore the chasm that was trapping me in limbo, a stretch of thick white clouds with a strong repelling force field that wouldn't let me cross over to the golden mansions in the distance. Though I could see other beings among the mansions going back and forth about their business, not one stopped to look in my direction. So I was surprised when, on my tenth day of poking at this force field, I looked up and saw a man watching me from one of the mansions in the clouds.

"Kubra!" the man called, waving and smiling.

"Hi," I said, unable to find the man's face in my memory.

"Look closely," he said, and then I saw his face clearly, the thick brows and piercing gaze.

"Father!" I wanted to jump into his arms but he was too far above me.

He smiled and waved again. "Soon you will be able to come here, when your mission on earth is complete, when you are released."

What did that mean? I thought of my ashes, saved by Mother in a jar. I thought of being entrapped by love and memory. I thought of Persephone being held by Hades against her will.

"What happened to you?" I asked. "Why are you here?"

"Money ritualists got my scrotum," he said and winced.

I stared at him, horrified, as he told me of his ordeal. Two years before my death, he'd gone to Lagos to interview for a high-paying job. The salary would change our family's fortunes, allow us to leave Kasar Lafiya for the southwest. From Lagos, he'd called Mother to say that the interview had gone well. He'd been hired and asked to start his new job the following week. To save money for moving expenses, he'd decided to travel home by bus instead of airplane. So at 5 a.m. he'd called Mother to say that he'd boarded a bus near Jibowu Park.

It was a misty morning, and the bus had made several diversions from its usual route. "To avoid bad traffic," the driver had claimed.

But before long, the passengers found themselves in a thick rainforest, with a dozen machete-armed men surrounding the parked bus, forcing them out and seizing their phones and valuables. Clearly, the driver had been part of the plot.

Before the passengers' eyes, the men repainted the bus and changed the license plate. The driver returned to the main road to pick up more unsuspecting passengers. And then, again, the ritual killers descended on them. No one could escape.

I told my father we'd all wondered how it had been possible for a bus and its passengers to vanish from the face of the earth. I confessed that I'd secretly thought he'd abandoned us, changed his name, married another woman, started a new family in Lagos along with his new job. I had become moody, nursing this hate and distrust.

He asked what had happened to me: why was I in limbo? As he listened to my story, I saw pain and sympathy on his face. I knew, if I could get to him in the clouds, I would have a shoulder to cry on, just like I'd had when he'd lived at home with us. Now, when I told him I didn't know who'd killed me, he closed his eyes and said in a broken voice, "Someday the whole truth will be revealed."

I felt sorry that I couldn't share my discovery about Father's unfortunate situation with Mother and Danladi. When I'd left them and headed again for the white space of my limbo, she was still explaining to my brother that angels had taken Father on loan.

In limbo there was a host of other people who, like me, had been forced from their bodies by bomb blasts, grenade explosions, and fire. They all wanted to reach their final home, and I, too, desired to enter into my house in heaven and find rest. But I could not locate the key.

In this place were blooming bougainvillea gardens. As I hovered along, admiring the shrubs, the brilliant pink petals reminded me of the blouse Aquamarine had been wearing in May, when she left the IDP camp and climbed onto the bus that would take her back to Enugu, back to her family. What a moment for her! I had hovered beside her, watching, as she sat in the last row, as she opened the center page of *G!* magazine and read the headline "Wonderful Attractions in Nigeria." She read about the Gorilla Camp on Obudu Cattle Ranch, of its birds, waterfalls, and beautiful landscape. She read about the joys of observing gorillas in their natural habitat. The photos were stunning, especially the pictures of the cascading waters.

I tried to remember the feel of tap water splashing against my palms. I tried to remember the smell of fried chicken, the feel of Danladi's little fingers scratching my scalp as he twisted my hair into knots, a game he called "plaiting your hair." Those fond memories trailed away, and I turned and looked at Aquamarine as she sat there, lost in thought, staring through the bus window at the rolling green hills. I didn't know what she was thinking about, but a tear leaked down her left cheek. I put out a hand to catch it, but it slipped through my hand and fell onto her pink cotton blouse, a dark blossom. I admired her ability to cry. How long it had been since I last felt tears trickle down my cheeks.

And then I thought of Grace, in America. In late November I had seen her sit down at the back of a classroom in her new high school in Miami. I was there, seated on a high stool, unseen by the class, while an elderly woman, her teacher, stood at the board, explaining the parts of a paragraph. Grace had grown three inches in the past year; and when the teacher called on her to read a passage aloud, it was obvious that she had added an American tick to her accent, yet she mixed her speech with a unique Hausa flair that made her voice very pleasing.

Later that day, I stood by as she ate lunch at the cafeteria with her new friends, all of them busy with their phones.

That evening, in celebration of a successful interim adoption order with the process of finalizing her adoption in full gear, Grace helped her new father prepare dinner. They ate mashed potatoes and gravy, boiled green beans and biscuits, and they drank oolong tea. I wondered if Grace would soon forget what *tuwo shinkafa*, *tuwo masara*, and *miyar rago* tasted like. Her new brother had rusty brown hair, pale skin, and bright blue eyes, while her sister had shiny black hair, olive skin, and dark brown eyes, and they seemed friendly and polite. When her new mother made a joke after dinner, Grace laughed with them. The dimples in her cheeks were as deep as ever, and her white teeth contrasted beautifully with her umber skin.

When she lay on her bed that night, she clutched a picture of her old family to her chest and soaked her pillow with tears. Then she got up, found a picture of her new family, and tucked it under her pillow.

And Gaddo. In the first week of December, I had hovered beside her as she sat inside the belly of a tin bunker on the margins of the Nigerian-Nigerien border. Sweat streamed down her face and she shivered in pain from her contractions. A few other abducted girls-turned-wives knelt beside her, helping.

"Push!" said the one who looked most experienced. She was clad in a charcoal black hijab.

Gaddo pushed. Paused. Breathed.

Another powerful contraction.

Gaddo pushed. Paused. Breathed.

Another powerful contraction.

Gaddo pushed. And out slid her newborn son.

While the rest of the girls helped with other chores, the girl in the black hijab cleaned Gaddo, cleaned Gaddo's son, wrapped the baby in an *atampa* cloth, and lay him in Gaddo's arms.

Gaddo was curled, exhausted, on a mat-draped platform bed. "What will you call him?" said the girl in the black hijab.

"Kyauta," said Gaddo. She smiled and looked in wonder at the baby cradled in her arms. Weeping with joy, she brought him to her breast and suckled him.

Safiya. I reached for a branch of bougainvillea and looked up toward the clouds. I had never seen Safiya since her passing, but I knew she was somewhere up there, in a corner for martyrs.

But where was my key? A gentle breeze wafted dew from the pink petals, splashing it onto the golden ground.

"You will not find your key there," someone said.

I looked up and saw Moshe standing a distance away in the clouds, his hands planted on his hips, a large smile on his face. I had first seen Moshe on the day I arrived in this limbo. Days later, I overheard that he had died in a gas chamber in Auschwitz at the age of eighteen. Moshe and I had never spoken to each other, so I was surprised now to hear his cheery voice addressed to me. He had long ago found his key, long ago found his home in one of the mansions.

"Where will I find mine?" I asked him.

"Only when your wishes find deep rest on earth."

"Are you sure that's how it works?" I said, and hoped my doubt didn't show.

He nodded and smiled again.

I smiled back and thanked him. I watched him ease his way down the crystal street, turn left, and disappear from sight. I thought of him in Auschwitz and wondered what his deepest wishes had been, at that moment when he had died in the gas chamber. I wondered how they had been granted. I thought, *Maybe I'll ask him some other day.*

I looked down at the pink bougainvillea by my feet. Mother had saved my ashes in a jar. How can I tell her to dig a grave and bury them?

PART THREE: 2017

KUBRA'S WISH

Inside Mother's kitchen, there was a tiny spider on the wall. Mother's cobweb broom must have missed it when she cleaned the kitchen the day before. I stood next to the spider, but it remained unaware of my ghostly presence, just like Mother did. I watched her eyes sweep past the spider as she spoke excitedly on the phone, but she did not notice it because it was just as brown as the kitchen walls. She said, "Major," in an endearing way as she pretended to rebuke him about the hot pepper in yesterday's *suya*. I smiled and nodded.

It was 6 p.m., and in a corner of the kitchen, the voice of a newscaster droned quietly from a small radio on the storage cupboard.

> . . . BREXIT: The Prime Minister of the United Kingdom to define divorce deal from the European Union in January 2017.
>
> "WHO ends ZIKV, the Zika virus, as a public health emergency of international concern in November, but epidemiologists continue research on the spread of the virus across the globe to mitigate risks of future epidemics.

> And in the US, the first black president of the United States leaves office after eight years in the White House and the forty-fifth president, the billionaire businessman, will be sworn in on January 20, 2017.
>
> And just before the break, here is the local news. Yesterday, on Saturday, January 7, at about 6:15 p.m., insurgents stormed a military base in Buni Yadi in Yobe State. Five soldiers feared dead. In the army's retaliatory strike, over a dozen militants were killed and. . . .

I was tired of hearing about one bomb blast after another, one massacre after another, but no major repercussions for the perpetrators. Insurgents? Militants? Would changing what the weasels are called suddenly stop their acts of terror? Why are soldiers being killed in their own space? What happened to military intelligence? I turned to Mother, who at that moment ended her call with Major Danjuma. She gave her *rago* stew one last stir, checked the rice pot, and turned off the stove. Dinner was ready, and Mother left for her room, perhaps to freshen up for dinner. I knew that her *rago* stew was heaven on earth. But I didn't have a seat at the dinner table anymore. My chair was now a waystation for folded napkins before Mother tucked them away in the storeroom. I didn't blame her or Danladi for that.

Shortly after, there was a knock at the front door. I wafted into the sitting room and watched Mother, clothed in a flowing silk turquoise blue *bubu,* open the door for Major Danjuma. They shared a brief hug and Major Danjuma joined Danladi in the sitting room while Mother set the table for dinner.

Danladi sat cross-legged on the couch, his eyes bright with delight, as he listened to Major Danjuma read to him one of the Hausa folktales from Rattray's translation of Maalam Shaihua's *Hausa Folk-Lore, Customs, Proverbs, Etc.*—a book from Father's small library collection, stored on the cabinet shelf below my trophies and photos. Most of the tales concluded with the refrain "Off with the rat's head."

Major Danjuma's voice was melodious as he read a story about a test of skill. A chief had three sons and, on a certain day, he decided to learn which one was the most skilled. The contest took place at the entrance of their house, where there was a very big baobab tree. All three sons were on horseback. As the first son's horse galloped toward the tree, the young man pierced the tree with his spear, creating a hole large enough for both horse and rider to pass through. The second son urged his horse into a trot, and the pair leaped over the tree without falling. But as the third son's horse galloped past the tree, the rider rooted up the baobab with his bare hands and waved it at his father and the applauding crowd.

Major Danjuma looked up and asked Danladi, "Which son had the best skill?" Then he narrowed his gaze and said conspiratorially, "Do you know, or do you not know? The story, the story."

And just before the major whipped out the closing refrain, Danladi piped his own twist of the line: "*Cire kan bera!*—Remove the rat's head!"

The two shared a laugh. The sight of them together, chatting and laughing, reminded me of how Father used to read stories from the same book to Danladi and me. Danladi was only a tot then. But I was always happy to squeal the refrain at the end of each story, and sometimes I wondered if rats would disappear from the planet. They seemed to lose their heads so often.

Now Danladi asked the major to read him the story about the origin of the spider, but Mother called them to the dinner table.

As they said grace, I hovered over them, then sat on the folded napkins. The three began to eat, and Major Danjuma praised Mother's stew. For a moment there was quiet. Then Mother asked Danladi, "Would you like Major Danjuma to be your new daddy?"

Danladi's eyes widened as he looked from Mother's face to Major Danjuma's and back to Mother's. "You always say that Father will come back soon. Are you giving up?"

"No," Mother said.

Danladi dropped his fork onto his plate. His eyes were filled with betrayal. He pulled back his chair and ran to his room.

Mother threw a sad, questioning gaze at Major Danjuma and dropped her eyes to her plate. She said nothing, focusing on the rice she was spooning into her mouth.

"We have to give him time," said Major Danjuma. "'Perhaps, another year."

Mother nodded but didn't look up from her plate. "Or maybe he's right." She dropped her fork in her plate. "I don't know. Sometimes I wonder, what if we get married and my husband, his father, returns? I'm sure I'll run mad."

Major Danjuma sat still at the table. His nods started slowly and became faster and more vigorous as Mother's words seemed to sink in. "Sadau, I understand," he said hoarsely. "I think it would help if we took a break from seeing each other. But if you change your mind, I will be waiting for you."

Mother nodded her thanks, her eyes bright with unshed tears.

"I'll take my leave now. Goodnight."

As the major headed for the door, Mother perched on the edge of her seat, looking as though she wanted to jump up and run into his arms. When he shut the door after him, she pushed her plate away and slumped into her seat. Staring off into space, she huffed, "I don't know if I should continue waiting for you, Anthony. Or whether I should move on. Why do you leave me in the dark?"

Father isn't coming back, Mother, I said. But of course, she couldn't hear me. I felt sorry for her. She must be racked with guilt. And I knew that Major Danjuma felt equally helpless. I'm sure he wanted to tell Danladi how much he loved Mother, how it would be an honor to become Danladi's new father, but he knew he couldn't speak and further upset the household. I wished there was a way to tell them all that Father was long dead and in his house in heaven. I wanted them to move on with their lives and not make a monument of his disappearance.

But there was nothing for me to do. I left her, vanished through the walls and into the night, sad to be so useless.

AQUAMARINE

Using a palm-frond broom, Aquamarine swept the stretch of plain red earth that surrounded their house. The markings she made resembled abstract ocean waves. It was a skill she had learned from the other girls in her junior days at boarding school. Now, as she stroked the earth in the early hours of the day, creating waves, listening to the jarring mix of birdsong and the swishing broom, her mind roamed free. Sometimes, it was caught in flash-forwards, riding new dreams, hopes, and aspirations. At other times it circled among flashbacks. Though eight months had passed since her bus had cruised into Enugu, she was still surprised that she was no longer a captive in a terrorist camp. As the bus had inched through highways and avenues to the motor park, she had noticed the city's orderly streets dotted with low- and mid-rise buildings, the people's attractive mix of European and African attire, and the faint hue of red dust on some of the house walls and fences. Enugu was different from Kasar Lafiya, with more tarred roads, more traffic jams, more bustling energy.

After disembarking, she had walked to her father's spare-parts shop at the Ogbete Main Market. There he was, a small man swimming inside a blue-and-white-striped *adire* shirt. He was expecting her: Sergeant had already called to tell him what had happened.

After welcoming her and asking a few questions about her abduction and escape, her father told her, "In April of 2015, after your Auntie Ijeoma told us you'd been abducted by terrorists, she canceled our debts and left Kasar Lafiya for Lagos with Ngozika, one of your cousins."

Aquamarine shook her head sadly and said, "I don't remember Ngozika very much, but I feel sorry for her." Then she smiled, and added, "Thank God I was abducted."

What had she been thinking, to make such a comment? Now that she had tasted freedom, the statement seemed absurd, yet the fact that her abduction had paved a way for her escape from her auntie's claws was undeniable.

But her father hadn't seen the humor. Instead, he'd stared at her as if she'd been brain-damaged by her ordeal.

Quickly, she said, "Don't worry, Papa. I'm not crazy. I'm just glad to be free from that woman," and she rattled off Newton's law of universal gravitation as proof. Still, he remained pale and uneasy, chewing his lower lip as he nodded.

Now she stooped and pulled out the few weeds that were in her path and swept them along. They were easy to pull because the dew had softened the soil.

That day of her return, she was glad her father had cared enough to lock the doors of his shop by 4 p.m. instead of the usual 5:30, and the two had hailed a taxi for the long ride to their house on the outskirts of the city. Aquamarine had admired the way the tarred roads folded like black seams into the green hills in the distance. Eventually the taxi stopped in front of a yellow square bungalow marked with red dust, and a young woman with lovely gapped teeth came out of the house to welcome them. Father introduced her as Nkechi, her mother's caregiver.

Inside, Aquamarine noted the sweet scent of lavender and sandalwood.

"It's the Isi brand," said Nkechi.

"And locally made," added Aquamarine's father with a nod of his head, "by a hardworking young man from Nkechi's clan."

When Aquamarine reached the door of her mother's room, she paused for a moment and watched her mother seated on the bed, gazing through the window, lost in her thoughts. She looked tired but tidy and neatly dressed.

"Mama," said Aquamarine.

Her mother looked up, squinted, and smiled. "*Aqua m ji n'anya*—My cherished Aqua."

Aquamarine fell onto her knees and buried her face in her mother's lap. She liked the rough feeling of her mother's palm against her fluffy afro. She took a deep breath, filling her nostrils with the musky smell of her mother's wrapper. When she finally sat up, her mother cupped her chin in her hand and said, "*Nnọọ n'ụlọ*—Welcome home."

The words Aquamarine had been waiting for forever. She had smiled but hot tears rolled down her cheeks unchecked.

Now she bundled up the litter into a bin bag at the end of her sweeping and thrust it into the metal drum at the corner set aside for burning rubbish. And as she walked back into the house, she admired the waves in the sand.

In the months she had spent at home, Aquamarine, with Nkechi's help, had taken over her mother's care: cooking, bathing, and feeding her; plaiting her hair. She worked on helping her mother use her limbs again. They had writing sessions, speech sessions, walking sessions. There was no real improvement in her mother's physical condition, and her mother's mind and memory were also slowly fading. Nonetheless, Aquamarine herself felt better. She began to laugh and smile more often. She began to treasure the little things that she had once taken for granted: clapping with excitement, spinning in place. And watching her mother's joy in her company brought her so much happiness.

PART THREE: 2017

• • •

The next month, February, on the Monday that marked the ninth-month anniversary of her return home, Aquamarine finished up a writing session with her mother and then said, "Now, Mama, it's time to exercise your legs."

When she leaned forward to lift her mother up, her mother gripped her arm and stopped her. "*Nsọ nwanyị*," she said, tugging at the hem of her daughter's skirt.

Aquamarine craned back to look at herself and saw a bloom of blood on the cloth. "*Hewoo! Ngozi, n'ikpeazụ!*—Blessing, at last!" she laughed. She felt an exhilarating rush, as if she'd crossed a finish line, catching the tape on her chest, winning the golden cup. She folded her hands and said reverently, "*Ndewo Mary!*—Hail Mary!" Now, no one would call her *yaro* or boy as Malam Hamzah had done at the camp, she thought.

Her mother beamed.

The next evening, as Aquamarine was feeding her mother bread mashed in hot cocoa, Nkechi brought her a little toiletry bag of period supplies. "Congratulations," said Nkechi. "You are a woman now."

Aquamarine liked the sound of those words, though they made her shy. But she also felt thankful for the delay that had saved her from marriage to Ahmad.

There was a knock at the main entrance door. "That must be your father," Nkechi said and hastened out of the room.

"She is a good woman," slurred Aquamarine's mother.

Aquamarine nodded and fed her mother the last bits of the food. Then she picked up the tray and headed for the kitchen. But when she stepped into the passage that led to the kitchen and the sitting room, she caught sight of her father and Nkechi whispering and caressing each other's cheeks beside the dining table.

When they saw Aquamarine, they dropped their hands but remained close together.

Unsmiling, she waited for an explanation.

"We plan to get married," her father said.

"What about Mama?" Aquamarine snapped.

"Hasn't she told you?" he asked.

Aquamarine shook her head, shocked. She dropped the tray on the dining table, turned away without speaking, and returned to her mother's room. Sitting on the bed, she said, "Mama, you told me Nkechi was a good woman. What is she doing with Papa while you and Papa are still married?"

Speaking with difficulty, her mother said haltingly, "My brain cells are dying. The doctor tells me I don't have long to live. I don't want to spoil the time we have together."

Aquamarine felt sorry for her mother, sorry for herself. She knew the disease had cheated her mother out of the best years of her life. She patted her mother's hand.

"Nkechi and your father have my blessing," said her mother.

Nodding, Aquamarine embraced her mother. She stared out the window at a large orange tree covered with tiny green fruit. By April or May, they would ripen, but for now they were certainly sour. Aquamarine wondered what her mother usually thought of as she sat looking out this window.

"Mama," asked Aquamarine, "are you afraid of dying?"

"No," said her mother slowly and with difficulty. "After these long years of battle, I welcome it."

Aquamarine remembered the moment when she herself had faced death: that moment when she didn't know if the police officers would help her escape from the suicide vest or if the men with the remote control would obliterate her. She had been afraid to die, even though her life had already been filled with rejection and abuse. She had chosen instead to cling to the hope that her mother would not reject her. She still didn't know what she would have done if her mother had.

Later that evening, Aquamarine's father ushered a stranger into their sitting room, introducing him as a government-sponsored reporter from Abuja. The man wore the thickest glasses Aquamarine had ever seen and carried his equipment inside a large black leather case that seemed to be almost too heavy to lift. He had heard Aquamarine's story from his contacts in Kasar Lafiya, and Sergeant had given him her contact address. Now he wanted to hear Aquamarine's version of her suicide-vest escape so that the government could document it as a success in the fight against terror.

During the conversation, the reporter mentioned the numerous options available for girls who had been directly affected by terrorism and its trauma. Aquamarine listened carefully as the reporter described a government rehabilitation camp in Abuja and the possibility that she might complete her education at the American University in Yola on a full government scholarship. She had no interest in any more camp experiences, but she was delighted by the idea of finishing her studies and getting on with her life.

The next evening, the national *News at 9* featured Aquamarine's story, which she watched in the sitting room with her parents. As the credits rolled, she told them that she planned to accept the offer to attend the American University in Yola. When her father suggested that she might gain more federal allowances if she chose the rehabilitation camp, she stared at him in disgust.

"I'm eighteen this year, Papa," she said. "Going on nineteen. I've lost one year of schooling already. My education is my independence. You should know that."

"Of course, you're right," he said, turning away his head in shame. After a few minutes of silence, he said goodnight and disappeared into his room.

"Mama," said Aquamarine when he was gone, "is Papa really my father? He's always choosing money over what's best for me. Or do I have a real father somewhere whom I don't know about?"

Her mother smiled. "There is no other father anywhere," she slurred. "I'm sure he wants what is best for you. But his approach is different. He thinks money solves everything."

Aquamarine didn't care much for her father's approach, but she didn't pursue the subject further. Instead, she changed the channel to the ongoing national singing talent competition. A boy representing Rivers State, who seemed to be about her age, was telling the judges he would sing Lionel Richie's "Hello." He was dressed fashionably in a fancy shirt and dark jeans.

After some small talk, the judges wished him good luck, and the boy beamed. When Aquamarine saw his prominent teeth, she shook her head. Grace would have nicknamed him "Teeth Apology," and she wouldn't have argued. But when the boy began to sing in his deep baritone voice, she instantly got goosebumps.

"He's the bomb! He's the bomb!" the three judges yelled.

In a flash, Aquamarine returned to that space when she'd been trapped inside a suicide vest. For a moment, she thought they meant that the boy, too, was strapped inside a vest and wondered why they were so elated. But when she saw the female judge dab tears from her cheeks and say, "Wow!" she grasped what they meant. She sighed in relief and, jumping up from her seat, started squealing along with the judges: "He's the bomb! He's the bomb!"

Her mother laughed. "Somebody wants to fall into the television!"

"Yes, Mama!" said Aquamarine. "Yes!" She laughed at herself for being so excited at the boy's performance and rebuked herself for writing him off as Teeth Apology.

The next performance, by a brother and sister duo from Abeokuta, paled against the first boy's performance. Even Aquamarine's mother said that their singing made her sleepy and hungry for roasted *ukwa*.

Aquamarine giggled, sat down, and wondered again at the judges' choice of the word *bomb*. A few months back, she would have been afraid to say the word. But that time felt like ages ago. Now she crossed her arms and, with her gaze on the TV, she reimagined herself as a new kind of bomb, one that would evoke tears of joy instead of tears of terror and destruction. Quietly, she said to herself, "I'm the bomb."

Three days later, as Nkechi was about to leave for the evening, Aquamarine's father received a phone call. It was for Aquamarine, an international number, and the moment she heard the cocky voice on the line, deep and strong and pleasant, she shouted, "Grace!"

Grace had seen Aquamarine's story on social media and had finally decided to call the number she had saved as "Aquamarine's runaway father." The two girls spoke for more than an hour, and before they hung up Grace begged Aquamarine to stay connected through social media.

But as Aquamarine gave the phone back to her father, she realized that she had no idea about how to operate a computer, despite her dream of becoming a professor of computer engineering. Before starting school in August, she would need help learning about social media and, if she were to stay connected to Grace, a temporary job to fund her phone calls.

"First and foremost," said her father, "we have to get you your own phone. These hour-long international chats between you and your friend cannot keep tying up the phone I dedicate to my trade."

"Papa, you and money," Aquamarine snickered.

As Nkechi lingered to listen, Aquamarine described the computer lab at St. Thomas Memorial School. It had tables, chairs, a chalkboard, boxes of chalk, a red-painted sign that said, "Computer Laboratory," but not one single computer. The man who had been contracted to supply them had spent the money on family holidays in Dubai and South Africa. Yet two of his daughters had attended their school, and nobody had held him accountable.

"That happens everywhere in Nigeria," said Nkechi.

"Our *fine* country," said Aquamarine.

But Nkechi knew someone who could help with computer training, social media, and maybe a job, if she were interested.

"Who and where?" asked Aquamarine.

"Ndubuisi," said Nkechi. "My clan member who produces the lavender and sandalwood scent that you love so much. He runs a cybercafé close by."

"Okay," said Aquamarine. Though she felt she should dislike Nkechi for taking her mother's place, she knew the woman was kind and helpful and hard to hate.

Two days later, Aquamarine walked down the street to Ndubuisi's cybercafé. Inside were thirty desktop computers lined up in neat rows, all in use by clients who had purchased hourly time slots, and a separate room at the back with a handful of people learning computer appreciation and coding. A small queue of people stood beside the receptionist at the door, waiting their turn for slots. Two men and two women were walking among the tables, available for clients who needed help.

When Aquamarine asked the receptionist if she could talk to Ndubuisi, one of the assistants walked over to meet her. He had a big smile on his face.

"Aquamarine," he said and shook her hand. "I am Ndubuisi."

"Hi," Aquamarine said, surprised. She hadn't seen him before. How did he know who she was?

"This is Isi Cybercafé," said Ndubuisi in a businesslike voice. He introduced her to the other staff, showed her the space's safety features, and then said, "Training starts now."

"Okay, sir," she answered.

Ndubuisi led Aquamarine to his office, where a desktop computer sat on a side table. Another sat on his desk, alongside his laptop. She took a seat at the side table, and Ndubuisi began the tutorial. His teaching style was engaging. He explained complicated ideas so simply that, by the end of the first session, she already felt like an expert. But she was puzzled by his distant manner. She had assumed he would be as friendly and open as Nkechi was. He was large and much taller than she was. His toned muscles, sculpted biceps and forearms, and big chest, which she found surprisingly attractive, made her hyperaware of her small frame. Her heart hammered in a way that made her feel breathless whenever he was near her. To keep her emotions in check, she convinced herself that his head was too big. *Yes, he has a big head,* she thought. Grace would have nicknamed him "Head Boy," and she would have agreed with her 100 percent.

But during lunch break, Ndubuisi sent a staff member out to buy Aquamarine a takeout meal of fried rice, fried chicken, and soda. While she ate, he sat down nearby and, as he finished his lunch, asked how she'd felt about the morning session. Now that she was chewing on the juicy chicken that he'd bought for her, how could she tell him that he was too serious and distant?

"Fine," she said instead.

"I thought you seemed a little distracted," he said.

Aquamarine looked at him and thought carefully before she spoke. "Perhaps I was thinking about some old school memories."

He ate a last bite. "You'll have to concentrate if you want to learn," he said. Smiling, he vanished with his takeout plate, and Aquamarine wanted to growl.

When Ndubuisi reappeared, he sat down at his desk, switched on his computer, and began to work on something of his own. Meanwhile, Aquamarine finished her food, got up to throw away her tray, and then sat back down, staring in every direction but his. There were still fifteen minutes left on her lunch break.

With his eyes focused on the screen, Ndubuisi suggested, "Walk around the place. Stretch your legs."

Aquamarine jumped up from her desk and went out to the cybercafé. The receptionist, a cheerful girl, apparently just a little older than Aquamarine, asked how the training was going and then asked Aquamarine about her camp experience. She said she'd seen news about her on TV and the internet, and Aquamarine asked to see the internet version.

The receptionist punched at the keyboard, and headlines filled the screen. She clicked on the first headline, and Aquamarine saw Sergeant with the defused suicide vest at his feet, saw herself clad in a black niqab with her eyes blanked out. She was glad her identity was protected in the photo and pleased to learn Sergeant's full name, which she read for the first time in the caption: "Heroes of the Day: Teenage Suicide Bomber Declines to Bomb IDP Camp, Sergeant Ono Osas Helps Detonate Bomb." Her name was mentioned in other headlines on the page. The contrast between her life then and her life now was clear. But the black shroud reminded her of the many girls who were still trapped in terrorist camps. She thought of the girls who had died in bomb blasts, of those forced to serve as human target practice. The brainwashing and suicide bombings, the rapes, the deaths in childbirth, the beatings: everything that the female body could be subjected to. Aquamarine thought about Safiya and Gaddo.

For the rest of the day, Aquamarine was quiet and focused. She was determined to soak up as much information as she possibly could.

After three weeks of coaching, Aquamarine had learned enough to work as a support instructor at the café. Ndubuisi surprised her with the congratulatory gift of an iPhone and told her she could start her new job immediately. When Aquamarine told him that she'd like to work for the next four months so that she could save money before school began in August, he nodded, then asked what her relationship with her father was like.

Aquamarine said, "Just okay." She was reluctant to speak. It seemed wrong to share family business with a new boss.

"I think he really cares for you," said Ndubuisi. "He's very protective of you."

Aquamarine hooted. "Tell me about it."

Ndubuisi did tell her something. He said that the day before her training had begun, her father had visited him in his café office and had warned him not to trouble his daughter with romance.

Aquamarine laughed.

Ndubuisi said, "In his own words, your father said, 'Make the training straightforward. My daughter has gone through a lot already. I don't want anybody to wound her with boyfriend-girlfriend relationship *nsogbu.*'"

"He said that?" Aquamarine was amazed. She'd never imagined that her father cared that much about her.

"If you tell him I told you what he said, I'll fire you before you even start work." Ndubuisi feigned seriousness, but then he smiled.

Aquamarine liked his smile. "Lips sewn up," she said.

She returned to her desk; but as she began to clear her things, she remembered to ask a question that had been on her mind since she started her training. "That first day I came to the café, how did you know I was Aquamarine?"

"Every other day I have another job," said Ndubuisi. "Before I open the café at 8 a.m., I deliver my scents to many homes, including yours. Through the window netting, I've seen you sweeping and dusting your sitting room. I've even seen you sniffing at some of my air fresheners."

"You spy on me?" Aquamarine asked, appalled.

"N—no," Ndubuisi said, with a look of fright. "I just see you. I—I do my business and go off to my next client."

Aquamarine felt sorry that he had never tried to speak to her on any of those encounters. Perhaps he was really all about business. She was disappointed.

"And Nkechi described you," he added.

Aquamarine nodded and returned to packing up her bag.

"But besides all that," said Ndubuisi, "when I drop by, your father is usually looking through his window to see who's on the porch. He never used to do that. But since you returned, he's always keeping watch. Perhaps to scare off people with whatever intentions."

Aquamarine had learned so much about her father since meeting Ndubuisi. And if all that he'd said about her father were true, then her father really did care for her. But he had a horrible way of showing it or hiding it.

Aquamarine thanked Ndubuisi for the iPhone and went home.

• • •

The first video Aquamarine made with her phone was of her mother. Before going to work, she asked her mother how she felt about the sunrise and started videoing as her mother burst into the Igbo version of the hymn "Songs of Praise the Angels Sang." Still videoing, Aquamarine sat beside her and sang along as her mother slurred the words: *"Abụ otuto ndị mmụọ ozi na-abụ. . . ."*

That night, her mother died peacefully in her sleep.

When Aquamarine awoke the next morning and went to check on her and make a new sunrise video, she discovered the body, stiff and cold.

She lay down beside the corpse and refused to budge, regardless of pleading by her father, Nkechi, or anyone else. As her tears dripped silently onto the pillow, she envisioned the long slow dying of the cells of her mother's body. No longer able to wave her arms with excitement. No longer able to shout for joy. No longer able to run and dance. She thought of the weight her mother had carried, dragging around that corrupted body for so many years.

Then Aquamarine imagined her own body shutting down—failing sight, dying limbs, damaged liver—cramping her spirit into an ever smaller space. She imagined death reaching out its hand to rescue her. A new freedom, but one that must follow the terms of the rescuer.

With such thoughts in her mind, she could be thankful that her mother had found relief, despite the coldness of death.

Dry-eyed, Aquamarine watched the undertakers arrive midmorning to carry her mother's corpse away.

Aquamarine's mother had asked to be buried on the day of her death, which would avoid the cost of mortuary fees. The burial plans had already been in place for months.

Afterwards, Aquamarine's father called Auntie Ijeoma to tell her about her sister's passing and burial. Through the speaker, an aghast Aquamarine heard her say, "Oh. At last. May Adannaya rest in peace. I will visit soon to pay my respects," and then ask, "Would Aquamarine like to come and spend time with me in Lagos, to take her mind off her mother's passing?"

Aquamarine's father looked over at his daughter. Aquamarine remembered that her auntie had never bothered to call and ask about her, not even after news about her ordeal was broadcast nationally. She said aloud, "Save your offer, auntie. I am fine where I am. Goodbye." Then she reached for the phone and pressed the "end call" button.

Her father chuckled. "Your auntie will be extremely angry. I doubt if anybody has had the guts to hang up on her before."

"There's a first time for everything, Papa," said Aquamarine.

"You remember your distant cousin Ngozika?" he asked. "The one your auntie took to Lagos after your abduction? Last month the girl ran back home to her aged parents. She now sells *okpa* at the RTC Holy Ghost Park."

"Did she say why she ran away?"

"There must have been a reason. Otherwise, she wouldn't have left a comfortable situation to hawk snacks at a motor park." Her father sighed. "Now I understand the mistake I made in allowing that woman to take you to Kasar Lafiya."

Aquamarine was glad to see him finally admit the injustice he'd done to her. Her respect for him was gradually being restored.

Every day, for a month after her mother's death, Ndubuisi visited Aquamarine at home during his lunch break. She was pleased, though he didn't say much. He would just sit for a while, ask how she was coping, encourage her to make videos, to vent her thoughts and emotions. Sometimes he would bring her takeout rice and chicken or pies. And at the end of the month, he brought her an envelope of cash, even though she had only worked for one day.

"Consider this a paid leave," he said when Aquamarine protested.

"I can't take this. I haven't worked enough," she said.

"That's okay," he responded. "Save it to buy your school supplies."

Reluctantly Aquamarine agreed, telling him that she was ready to go back to work the next day. She said she needed to keep herself occupied, to stop moping and worrying. Though Ndubuisi encouraged her to take her time, she was adamant.

Later that evening, as Aquamarine was ironing a cotton dress for work, Nkechi, now her stepmother, walked in after her nursing shift at the local hospital. She admired the bright colors of the dress.

Aquamarine said, "I told Ndubuisi that I wanted to start work so he wouldn't waste his money and pay me again at the end of the month when I didn't do anything."

"Waste, *kwa*?" Nkechi said. "I'm not sure Ndubuisi would miss any money he spends on you. You wouldn't believe he has a wealthy family, but at twenty-four years of age, he's done well on his own and keeps a very low profile. He's not someone who makes noise, even when it concerns his emotions. But I think he likes you a lot."

Aquamarine smiled. She enjoyed hearing that Ndubuisi liked her, and she hoped it was true because she liked him, too, and she didn't know how to calm her heart when he was near. "I'm glad you are my new mother," she said to Nkechi.

"I count myself lucky to have you as a daughter and to have a new family with you and your father," Nkechi replied.

Early the next morning, just before leaving for work, Aquamarine visited her mother's room to create a final sunrise video, just as she would have done if her mother had been sitting on the bed, looking through the window. Afterwards, she sat on the bed, in her mother's place, and gazed out at the tree. The oranges had become larger and many were patched with yellow, promising sweetness. Inside, the room was scented with orange fragrance and with the lavender and sandalwood Isi air freshener hanging in the corner.

As Aquamarine walked down the street to work that morning, Grace phoned. The friends chatted about living parents, dead parents, and new parents; about old classmates, new siblings, and new lovers;

about old dreams, new dreams, and new goals; about Kubra, Safiya, and Gaddo. Aquamarine hung up just before she entered the cyber-café but then quickly sent Grace a text:

> AQUAMARINE: I really enjoyed chatting with you.
> GRACE: Me too. Take care. Bye.
> AQUAMARINE: Bye.
> GRACE: Stay safe.
> AQUAMARINE: Chat soon.

GADDO

Under the blazing late April sun, Gaddo leaned over the small fireplace beside her husband's tin bunker and stirred a pot of boiling root soup. She heard her baby begin to cry inside the bunker and hurried to finish her task, lifting the pot from the fire with her bare hands and setting it on the ground. She spooned some soup onto a metal plate already mounded with *tuwo shinkafa* and covered the pot with another plate. With the food in one hand, she rose and moved toward the door. But just before she lifted the latch, she looked around. No one was in sight, so she spat into the soup and stirred it with her forefinger. Then she went inside.

Chinks in the latch allowed fingers of sunlight to stream into the bunker. Making her way down the steps, Gaddo set the plate on the floor beside her husband, Ahmad, who was seated on the raffia mat draped over their plywood platform bed. He was holding the baby, Kyauta, and now she took the child from Ahmad's arms and patted him to stop his cries. Ahmad offered to feed Kyauta some of his food, but Gaddo ignored him, instead sitting in the corner and pushing Kyauta's mouth onto her nipple under her blouse. She didn't care that he wouldn't suckle.

Gaddo watched Ahmad gobble his food, then lick his fingers one by one. After his plate was clear he began to tell Gaddo about his plan to send Kyauta to one of the almajiri schools in Kano. Gaddo eyed his tattered left ear and cursed him under her breath: *He's not even your child!* She swore to herself that Kadir's son would never enter any school that would relegate him to the profession of begging on the streets.

Ahmad's big phone rang, and he dropped his plate onto the floor. In a rasping voice, he started complaining to the caller about late deliveries, then hung up. He jumped to his feet and hurried up the steps, then dashed back, grabbed his two smaller phones from the mat, and left.

Moments later, Gaddo heard the sound of a helicopter. She set Kyauta on the bed to play by himself while she climbed the steps and lifted the latch to peek outside. Bundles of supplies were dropping haphazardly from the helicopter. She noticed that the man who was pushing them out had pale skin, and the wind from the rotors was whipping his sandy hair every which way. Soon the chopper flew away, and she watched Ahmad, who was standing among a group of other men and speaking to someone on his phone. His croaky voice was expressing gratitude. When he finished the call, he and the others began to lug the supplies to a nearby storage bunker.

Who were these people that Ahmad spoke with on his phone? All she knew is that they were wealthy enough to own or rent helicopters and deliver numbers of sophisticated weapons and bags and bags of food.

Suddenly she noticed that Kyauta was silent. When she glanced back at him, she saw that he was sucking on one of Ahmad's dirty shirts. She snatched it from his mouth and flung it into the corner. When the child began to cry, she lifted him into her arms and planted kisses on his mouth, his cheeks, his hands, patting him and babbling at him until he stopped crying and started laughing.

GADDO

• • •

That night, Gaddo stayed awake as Kyauta sighed in his sleep beside her on the bed. The night air was cool and dry, and the bunker's tin walls held in the chill. For several days Kyauta had been suffering from a rash on his face, and her worry about him had disrupted her sleep. Finally, though, the spots had begun to fade, since she had started dabbing breast milk on them. As she studied his face, the hump on his small nose always reminded her of Kadir's hooked nose.

Ahmad slipped into the bunker. He dropped his rifle, and Gaddo heard it clang against the motorcycle parked against the wall. In the darkness, he reached for her and lifted her wrapper. She allowed her mind to go blank when he entered her, as she always did. For five minutes their bed creaked, and soon he was asleep and snoring. She lay awake beside him, cursing the day of her abduction. She wondered if she'd ever see her mother again, hear her mother's low-pitched voice; she wondered if her mother were even still alive. She thought about Kadir and his searching voice, the sound of his laughter, his smile. But Ahmad's snoring cut into her thoughts. She swore that she would find a way to get away from him and his tin prison. With that vow in her mind, she forced herself to sleep.

At 3 a.m. Gaddo jerked awake to the sound of bullets hissing, crackling. And then the bombs began to drop, each explosion shaking the ground, the bunker walls, the objects inside. Gaddo curled up tight, clutching Kyauta to her bosom, patting him frantically to pacify him and muffle his cries.

Ahmad, meanwhile, was perched on the steps, peering through the chinks in the latch, his rifle poking through a slit. Now and again he fired.

Gaddo was furious. If the military pilots saw him shooting, their bunker would become the next bombing target. "Selfish! Thoughtless!" she muttered to herself.

As the bombardment continued, one of Ahmad's small phones rang. It lay next to Gaddo on the bed, but she refused to hand it over to him. Cursing, he dropped his rifle and rushed down the stairs to grab the phone, then hurtled back to his position. Shouting and rasping, he chastised the caller for failing to separate two bags of explosives and a trunk of grenades from the food they'd stowed in the storage bunker. If a bomb fell on those explosives, the group would be out of food and ammunition for weeks.

Gaddo longed for the bombing to stop, but she also wanted all of the terrorists to be caught or obliterated. So when a bomb landed close to their bunker and the vibration threw Ahmad from his perch onto the floor, she grinned, listening to him cower in the corner, yawping and swearing in the name of his ancestors. But the raid was nearly over. After a few more minutes of noise, the planes flew away and a heavy silence descended. Ahmad lifted the latch and peered into the sky and into the woods. Hearing and seeing nothing, he opened the door and dashed outside. Seconds later Gaddo heard the snap of another bunker's latch and Ahmad arguing with some men.

In the silence Kyauta had fallen asleep in Gaddo's arms. Now she lay him on the bed, searched the mat for a phone, and found the biggest one beside her. Using it as a flashlight, she located a small phone at the foot of the bed. Ahmad's latest call had given her the germ of an escape plan.

By the phone's light, Gaddo looked around the bunker, noting the unlit kerosene lamp, the matchbox, the container of gasoline for Ahmad's motorcycle. *If this place explodes, the men will blame the military,* she thought. She picked up her sleeping child and leaned forward so that she could balance him on her back, binding him in place with a wrapper. She picked up the lamp, the matches, the fuel, then climbed the stairs and peeked outside. Everything was silent. Stealthily she lifted the latch and stepped outside. For a moment she stooped over her little fireplace, glancing around, alert to any movement. The bold moon looked lonely and mournful in the black sky. She noticed that the bombs had rooted up a few small trees and saw craters in the clearing. Carefully she inched her way to the storage bunker. Now she could hear Ahmad in the distance, arguing with a few other men about who had died during the raid.

A few trees were still smoldering, and the smell of burnt grass was strong. With her heart thumping, Gaddo set down her materials and lifted the latch of the storage bunker. Then she opened the gasoline can and splashed fuel onto walls and bundles. She lit the lamp and threw it into the bunker, along with the gasoline can.

By the time the explosions began, she was a few meters into the forest.

At first light, the sky shimmered with gray and black clouds. Gaddo was sure she had covered thousands of meters, running almost as fast as the sprinter she had once been. As far as she could tell, none of the men had caught up with her.

Then the phone rang. She looked at the screen: it was a caller named "M," with the image of a quarter moon and three stars. She didn't answer, and the phone stopped ringing. But the noise had startled Kyauta, and he began to cry. Gaddo twisted an arm behind herself and patted his bottom, and he soon rested his head against her shoulder, awake but calm. She hurried forward but had taken only a few steps when the phone rang again. She ignored it. But as she strode on, she scrolled through the phone's contact list and saw more than three hundred names. She wondered which numbers belonged to the people who'd sent the helicopter supplies to the camp. Her plan was to hand the phone to the police. With so many contacts, they'd be sure to track down all the terrorist sympathizers in the country, no matter their position or importance. Then the abductions would end.

Gaddo switched off the phone to save the battery and tucked it under the wrapper knot on her chest. Moments later, she came to a crossing, where the road she'd been following forked into two paths. She had no idea where either led. Her instincts pressed her go left, but that path looked deserted and had less stunted and scattered trees and shrubs, the kind of place where terrorists would tuck away their camps. So instead she took the righthand path, hoping to meet villagers who could help her. After a few kilometers, she came upon a hut, the first sign of habitation since she'd left the camp. It was surrounded by dwarf acacia shrubs. But as she drew closer, the shapes of the shrubs shifted, and men and motorcycles came into full view. She knew these men.

Gaddo stopped, and Ahmad said, "Where's my phone?"

Gaddo chewed her lip. Why hadn't she taken the other path? But she knew another group of men might have been waiting there as well.

She pulled out the phone and flung it at Ahmad. She didn't care if the screen broke or if she received a bullet in the back of the head. She was ready for the worst. She spun on her heel and began to retrace her steps. As she walked back to the camp, she said under her breath, "Tomorrow is another day to plot, if I live to see tomorrow."

GRACE

July 22, 2017

Dear Diary,

Trip to Disney World: postponed!
Instead, Mom, Jake, Amal, and I join Dad in a flight from Miami to Santa Rosa Beach. Dad has to meet with some of his business associates tomorrow morning. To make up for the canceled trip, Dad promised us not just a trip to Disney World next summer but a 7-night western Caribbean cruise.
Awesome!

Grace xxx

July 22, 2017

Hey, Diary,

We arrived at Seaside, Santa Rosa Beach, at 4:10 p.m. after a 45-minute ride from the airport.
The humidity is crazy.
If blood could boil. Yikes!

Grace xxx

PART THREE: 2017

July 23, 2017

Dear Diary,

Dad's meeting went well this morning. And yay, it's 4:00 p.m. Our beach time!

Santa Rosa Beach is a huge span of aquamarine water.

Thoughts about my friend Aquamarine and her power sprints dashed through my mind as we crossed from the gazebo and started walking down the flight of stairs that led to the white beach. It's been so nice chatting with her since we've reconnected.

I pray that Gaddo and the others have finally escaped those wretched kidnappers.

On the sand Dad and Mom lounge on big blankets under beach umbrellas and sip coconut margaritas sans tequila, and chat with some writers who are attending the Seaside Writers Conference, while Jake and Amal are busy building a sandcastle.

I am drawn to the water. The ocean is like a large green belt that links America to Africa. I walk straight into the cool water until it swallows my feet. Every time a wave swooshes past my legs to kiss the white sand behind me, the water flares up my calves, my knees.

"Aquamarine," I call out to the ocean, but the remaining words in my heart cleave to the roof of my mouth. Then, on the beach, I write my seventeenth poem, poems that I will never show anyone I know, poems that I think would get better if I take a poetry course when I attend college. This is how I escape to my world.

AQUAMARINE

But this beach at Seaside,
call her Pristine.
She sports a minty belt

that binds her azure skirt
to her white sandy blouse.
You wonder:
is her prime pleasure,
every time you meet her,
to catch your breath, shove it
under her thrashing sash,
and render you speechless?
And momentarily,
when she pities you
and releases your breath,
out of your mouth tumbles gasps,
and acclamations
in praise of her.
Would you really blame her?
You are knee-deep
in her crystal green waters
when you realize
she is chanting an invocation to you,
Penman of Santa Rosa:
leap,
thrash,
break,
wash.
Peppered with a sacrifice of fossils,
pink-white snail shells, periwinkles,
and thunder-blue sea urchins,
she cracks her crest against your chest,
ecstatic to entwine her arms about you,
brush your hair with her salt-tipped fingers and
splash bubbles in your face, and
you become a butterfly in her dark blue deeps.
Rogue beach, breath rogue, steals still,
while a castle of sand fashioned with hands
and sun and sweat,
and tingling laughter,
rises and crumbles.
The heavy-eyed sun winks
yellow fire and pink at the wet beach
and the Seaside scribes peg their feet
into the crumbly white sand,

and their small talk kneads the whispers
of the aquamarine ocean waves that intone
buenos noches to Santa Rosa
and belt her blue skirt
with white froth.

Grace xxx

July 23, 2017

Dear Diary,

After dinner, we return to our cabin at the Seaside Resort. It's 7 p.m., and I take a quick shower, then play two rounds of cards with Jake and Amal. Jake wins both. LOL.

Now he begins the harmless card tricks he learned from a classmate at school. He's good at them. That's why Mom nicknamed him Magic Fingers, but Amal and I call him the Wizard of the Cards and Dad tells him he should audition for America's Got Talent. This is how one trick goes: he lightly brushes the deck with the tips of his fingers and the cards become see-through plastic. He grins at our surprise. I notice that his rusty hair looks a shade darker under this dull yellow lamplight.

He's such a little darling. I think Simon Cowell would give him a golden buzzer.

With his sunny smile, no one would guess that at eight years old he had already passed through three different foster homes across different states here in the US. Mom and Dad intend to end that trend of foster-home trotting and give him a warm and proper home.

Grace xxx

July 23, 2017

Dear Diary,

During our fifteen minutes of family night devotion, Mom reads from the Book of Matthew, chapter 6, verse 33, and explains that the Kingdom of God is a place where life overcomes death and light rules supreme.

I pray for life for Mom, Dad, Amal, Jake, and me.

I pray for the light of wisdom, understanding, and love.

Grace xxx

July 23, 2017

Nighty-night, Diary.

It's 9:30 p.m.

Amal and I share a room with separate queen beds. Usually, once she settles on her bed, she falls fast asleep. But tonight she kept tossing and turning, and I sat up and asked her what the problem was.

"I am hungry for basbousa," she says. "Before the war in my home country, my yamo used to make basbousa, and I'd eat plenty."

My dear sister Amal, only six when the war in Syria broke out in 2011. That was when she lost both parents. A couple of years later she got adopted by Mom and Dad. She's usually very quiet and almost never speaks about her past. She has no idea how to make basbousa, she confesses. This is the first time I have heard the word basbousa, so I did a quick internet search on my phone. We need nuts, flour, plain yogurt, coconut, and sugar to bake the sweet, sticky, moist Syrian dessert, and the method is easy. I confide in Amal that she is not alone. Sometimes, I also have cravings for masa, Hausa pancakes made from rice. I suggest that when we get back home, we ask Mom and Dad to include basbousa and masa in our food roster. They love variety. Amal got excited when I proposed that she and I might teach Mom,

Dad, and Jake how to add a flavor of Damascus and Kasar Lafiya to our new home in Miami. I'm glad that she's excited and I'm hopeful that our bonding over diverse foods will create stronger sisterly and familial bonds.

Soon I hear her gentle snores.

As my head hits my pillow, before sleep claims me, my thoughts are filled with memories of Santa Rosa Beach and its aquamarine waters.

I'm glad Dad brought us here. I feel so rested, just thinking about the beach and breathing the seaside air. For once, I'm not mourning my home in Nigeria.

Signing out for the night.

Grace xxx

KUBRA'S TEETH

At age nine, Danladi received excellent marks on his common entrance examinations and was accepted into the Government Technical College in Kasar Lafiya. He said he wanted to learn about motor mechanics and become a mechanical engineer.

Early in my brother's first term, the principal introduced the school's new physical education teacher, Mr. Bako, during Friday-morning assembly. As soon as Danladi saw the man, he froze. I was hovering beside him, and I knew why: it was the man who had invaded our house, the man with the centipede scar across his left cheek, now with a fake name and a trimmed beard.

The first class Mr. Bako taught involved hunting with rifles. He asked the boys to shoot at cardboard targets cut into the shape of a man and a woman. On the man he wrote the letter *K* and told the boys, "K is for Kafir."

I was furious. Kafir meant *unbelievers, infidels.*

At dinner that evening, Danladi forgot to tell Mother who Mr. Bako really was. Instead, he excitedly described the class, including the targets tagged with *K* for Kafir.

Mother was angry, and the next morning, after dropping off Danladi, she reported the matter to his principal. The principal called in Mr. Bako and asked if the allegation were true. Mr. Bako said the letter *K* could stand for anything and mentioned that he owned a dog named Kafir.

The principal advised Mother to stop overreacting. She apologized to Mr. Bako and left.

During the next week's class, Mr. Bako taught the boys wrestling and tackling. He paired them and taught them what moves to make against each other. Some of the boys got bloody. Danladi was paired with his friend Jonah, and Mr. Bako showed the boys how to give someone a killer punch. When he asked Danladi to practice, Danladi froze, his eyes fixed on the centipede scar, his brow knotted in a frown.

So Mr. Bako told Jonah to practice the killer punch on Danladi. At first, Jonah refused, but Mr. Bako encouraged him, promising to help. He held Jonah's hand, guided it forward, and, like lightning, the punch landed on Danladi's neck. My brother crashed to the ground. "Stand up and fight back," Mr. Bako yelled, and soon the other boys were echoing him. Ashamed, Danladi got up and headbutted Jonah in the stomach. Jonah groaned, caught Danladi around the waist, and elbowed him. Wresting himself free, Danladi rammed a foot in Jonah's back. The boy fell face-forward into the sand.

Mr. Bako hailed Danladi as the champion of the day. All of the other boys shook hands with him and called him "Small but Mighty" because he was the youngest in the class.

When Danladi stretched his hand toward Jonah, his friend gave him a bear hug and called him "my best friend."

I liked that the boys took the wrestling competition in good spirit, but I couldn't understand why Mr. Bako wanted Danladi to become a fighter. I hoped he wasn't planning to recruit these boys into the weasel pack.

When Danladi got home, Mother asked about the bruises on his neck and face. He didn't tell her about the rough tackles Mr. Bako had taught them. Perhaps he didn't want her to visit the school and embarrass herself again.

But the next morning he was limping, and Mother made him confess.

Outraged, she stormed into the principal's office, shouting, "I've already lost a daughter. I'm not ready to lose my son. If that man doesn't know how to handle children, he shouldn't be teaching them."

The principal promised to ask Mr. Bako to tone down the roughness, but he made it clear that the teacher couldn't be sacked. Mr. Bako had high connections in government, and they had arranged his employment at the school.

Mother stormed away.

After work, Mama Lakhmi stopped by for a visit, and Mother explained the situation. She said she now planned to transfer Danladi to another school, perhaps one of the government colleges, even if that meant the boy would have to stay in a boardinghouse. Anything to get him away from that scar-faced man.

I was sitting on the floor beside them, and I scowled at Mama Lakhmi when she said that Mother was probably overreacting. But Mother didn't budge. She seemed determined to move Danladi to another school, and I was determined to stay close by. Neither of them knew how close they were to danger, as embodied by Mama Lakhmi and Mr. Bako.

Later that night, a few minutes past midnight, Mother heard noises at her window—faint footfalls, a splash against the outside wall. As the odor of petrol rose, she grabbed her flashlight, flung open the curtains, and shone her beam onto two men. One was Mr. Bako, with a small container of gasoline in his hand. She screamed, "Thief!" and both men fled.

Early the next morning Mother reported the incident, and the police, with Major Danjuma at their head, went on a search for Mr. Bako. After three days they trailed him to Mama Lakhmi's house and discovered a stash of sophisticated weapons. The pair leaped onto

Mr. Bako's motorcycle and sped away, but a police bullet caught Mama Lakhmi and she fell.

As the chase continued, Mr. Bako sped around a curve and crashed into an oncoming bread van, flipping over three times before crashing to the roadside in a heap. He broke his neck and spine and died on the spot.

Mother was shocked to learn the truth about Mama Lakhmi. Nonetheless, she visited her at the hospital.

"I'm sorry," croaked Mama Lakhmi.

Mother just stared at her.

"The day Kubra died," said Mama Lakhmi, "I was sent to visit you to make sure the intruders would find you at home."

"Are they the ones who killed my daughter?" Mother asked.

Mama Lakhmi chewed on her lips.

"The police never found out who parked the car with explosives across from my house," Mother said, "but Kubra must have known, and they thought it was wise to silence her, wasn't it? Or was she just unlucky to be at the wrong place at the wrong time?"

Mama Lakhmi looked away from Mother, and her lips trembled when she said, "They don't tell me everything. Only the assignments they want me to carry out."

"Why do you work for them?"

"Maybe I believed too much in their cause."

Mother shook her head.

"Whatever happens," said Mama Lakhmi, "do not travel to Birnin Haske any time soon. Men plan to ambush your vehicle, capture you, and take you to a forest camp, where you will be tortured and humiliated every day. This has been their plan for some years now."

"Why are you telling me this?" Mother asked.

"I feel guilty about Kubra."

Mother stared at her for a long while. Then, without another word, she left Mama Lakhmi's bedside and returned home to be with Danladi. I remained in the hospital room and watched Mama Lakhmi howl and struggle for breath.

She died that night. I watched her spirit slip out of her body. When she saw me, she didn't say a word. She just floated away in the opposite direction.

The following week, Major Danjuma called Mother on video chat after work, and informed her that due to the recent findings about Mama Lakhmi and her connection with a terrorist group, the case about my death had been reopened and an updated verdict given. The two bearded men who had initially been charged with intimidation were subjected to further interrogation and charged with committing and assisting to commit acts of terrorism, for driving a vehicle loaded with explosives—along with two other men who had been dishonorably discharged from the military years back and were now discovered to be sympathizers of insurgents—for helping those who fired the grenade. They were liable, upon conviction, to life imprisonment. However, with artful counsel from their lawyers, the men accepted a plea deal and requested to join the "Operation New View," a program established by the Birnin Haske community chief to rehabilitate and reintegrate repentant militants into the society. The court rendered its judgment in their favor.

Hovering back and forth from the window to the couch, I was shocked at how easily the weasels who had caused so much pain and loss were rewarded for "repenting."

Mother was seated on the couch in the sitting room with a photo of me and my friends in her hand. She brushed my image with her thumb, smiled sadly, and said, "I was hoping that we would finally get legal justice for Kubra, but apparently, we are living in a slaughterhouse. The regulators do not care for the needs or well-being of the *animals* as long as profit and corruption range free."

Major Danjuma leaned forward in his seat such that his face filled the screen of Mother's phone. "I don't care if I get punished or lose my job for my personal views," he muttered, gritting his teeth in silent fury and frustration. "I know the rehabilitation program has its merits, but I think the judgment is a mockery of justice."

I agreed.

"I will call again if there is any further news," the major said.

They said their goodbyes and ended their chat. Mother returned the photo to the shelf and tramped into her room.

I hovered in front of the shelf and continued to look at the photo. There I stood in the center, smiling broadly, holding the fifth cup we had won as a team, flanked by Aquamarine, Gaddo, and Grace. I remembered that after my accidental fall, I hardly smiled because I always felt too shy to show my chipped incisor, but not when I had this golden cup in my hands.

The framed photo that sat beside it, the newest addition to the collection, was of Aquamarine holding a golden cup, with Safiya and Gaddo on her right side and Grace on her left. I was glad that Mother had gotten the photo of the girls and fulfilled my goal of having photos of six trophies for Red House gracing the shelf. But I was missing from the photo and those responsible for my absence were somewhere, living.

I frowned and reached for the photo. I wanted to smash the glass, tear the picture into tiny bits, and feed the pieces to those who had caused my absence, but my hand went through the picture, unable to grab it. Not even a swooshing sound of rushing air accompanied the stroke of my hand. I yowled.

Thoughts of fresh air and bright skies flashed in my head and immediately I found myself hovering above the roof of the house. Dark clouds mapped the skies. Gusty wind set off small eddies of dead leaves and dust along the street, and used cellophane bags and pieces of old newspapers were floating in the wind. The first few drops of rain dripped right through me and splattered on the aluminum roof. There were a couple of rusty spots, though no holes had formed. Soon the heavy rain lashed against everything in its path. I didn't move, I didn't get wet. I just watched the rain continue its torrential lashing.

• • •

St. Thomas Memorial School had been rebuilt, and a celebration had been scheduled for October 3. It would feature many of the girls who had escaped abduction.

But a week before the event Mother received a letter stating that the former principal would continue as the school's principal, meaning that she would step down from her role as acting principal and resume her role as vice principal. She would not be promoted.

Mother was sad all day. At one point she considered taking her case to the governor and the Ministry of Education at Birnin Haske. But then she remembered Mama Lakhmi's advice—"Don't travel to Birnin Haske anytime soon"—and decided to let the matter rest.

She also had a new idea, and during dinner that day she discussed it with Danladi. Perhaps, she told him, she should open a private school and become her own boss.

Danladi thought the idea was great. But, as Mother explained, success would be an uphill battle. She would need community support. And then there was the challenge of funding. Worse still was the ongoing issue of terrorist attacks. Danladi agreed but remained enthusiastic, telling Mother that whatever she decided had his full support. I sat in my old seat at the table and nodded my support, too, even though I knew neither Mother nor Danladi could see me.

Aquamarine was a first-year computer science student at the American University of Nigeria in Yola when she attended the commemoration day at St. Thomas. She came with Ndubuisi and her parents, and Ndubuisi had driven them in his black Range Rover, saving them the hassle of a crowded bus ride. Many of her classmates, who had found their way home or been rescued by the military, were also there with their loved ones. Even Grace took part via video chat for a couple of hours. The girls hugged each other, sharing their stories and their goals.

The governor attended the ceremony, and during the festivities the director of the Ministry of Education announced that Mother would be the new principal. Confused, she told him about the letter she'd received. The director explained that his secretary's signature had been forged and the culprit caught. Relieved, Mother accepted the position and thanked everyone for their support. I stood a bit apart from the crowd, smiling as they applauded.

As people broke into smaller groups, eating, drinking, and chatting. Gaddo's mother, along with Amina, Amina's parents, and her little daughter Celine, asked if anyone had news of Gaddo. Aquamarine told them what she knew and said her friend had been married to a rough man and sent to another camp. She encouraged the family to stay strong. But Gaddo's mother stepped away from the throng and sat by herself, her eyes distant.

Safiya's mother wept when she heard what had happened to her daughter. She didn't stay till the end of the party. Other parents and guardians with missing girls also wept, though they were glad for the girls who had escaped.

Late that afternoon as the event wound up, while Ndubuisi and her parents walked toward his car, Aquamarine caught sight of Danladi standing at the end of the serving table. She hailed him joyously, as if he were her own little brother, and hugged him. He was all dressed up in a forest-green kaftan, and she noticed five charred, cracked teeth hanging from his collar. She asked about them.

"Kubra's teeth," he explained. "I strung them onto her old shoelace this morning so I could bring a piece of her to the party."

"That's a special thing to do," said Aquamarine. "She must be proud of you."

Danladi grinned as Aquamarine reached out and touched each tooth gently, one after the other, with her eyes closed. On her finger glittered the diamond engagement ring she had received from Ndubuisi just before starting college. It sparkled like fire in the light of the setting sun. They hoped to tie the knot after her graduation.

When she opened her eyes, she looked past Danladi and stared straight into mine. "Kubra," she whispered. "Sand."

In that fleeting second, I was sure she had seen me hovering over a mound of sharp sand, left over from the recent construction projects, a short distance away. Then she shook her head, as if she were coming out of a trance, and looked squarely at Danladi.

"Have you buried her?" she asked.

"No," he replied. "Mother is saving her ashes in a jar."

"I think Kubra deserves a proper burial in the ground, in a place that she can call her own," Aquamarine said thoughtfully.

Mother, who had just said her goodbyes to the governor and the director, stepped forward. "Lately I've have been thinking the same thing," she said. "But I wasn't sure. I guess, in life, sometimes we just must press on no matter how dark the road ahead appears to be. Thank you for convincing me. We'll give her a proper burial tomorrow, at first light." Mother took Danladi's hand in hers.

"Mami," said Danladi. "I've also been doing some thinking. I know Major Danjuma will make a good new dad. You always smile more when he visits. And he tells nice folktales."

Mother beamed. "That makes two of us. I'm sure he'll be glad when we tell him. I'll ask him to join us for Kubra's burial tomorrow."

Aquamarine hugged them both. "And I'll be there with my family, before I go back to Yola."

I wrapped my arms around all three of them, but of course they didn't know that.

I would finally enter my own house in heaven in the morning.

ACKNOWLEDGMENTS

Thanks to Robin McLean for choosing *Fine Dreams* as the winner of the 2023 Juniper Prize for Fiction and giving voice to the myriads who have been scorched by terrorism.

Thanks to the University of Massachusetts Press for publishing the book; to Courtney Andree, the bearer of good news; and to the editing and marketing team at the press, including Rachael DeShano and Mary Dougherty. Many thanks to Dawn Potter for her wonderful editing.

Special thanks to my family: Clifford (Dad, of blessed memory), Stella (Mum), Loretta, Rexford, Sandra, Paul Ekwere, Amaka, and a host of nephews and nieces—Chinedu, Ebus, KK, Miss O., Phils, and Debs. Your incredible support is the best! Lots of love!

Thanks to Knismeta, who edited an earlier draft of *Fine Dreams*. Much gratitude to Elizabeth Bowen for her awesome proofreading, Dr. Jill Patterson for her legal insight, and Tobi Abraham for reading. Thanks to faculty, colleagues, and friends in the University of Mississippi's MFA program and Texas Tech University's English/creative writing doctoral program for workshopping parts of the novel.

ACKNOWLEDGMENTS

A version of the chapter "Aquamarine" won the 2020 Bondurant Prize for fiction at the University of Mississippi, and a version of the chapter "Kubra's Errand" was a finalist in the 2021 Cascade Writing Contest.

Thanks to the University of Mississippi Graduate School for the 2019 summer research grant that enabled me to visit Nigeria.

Thanks to the members of my MFA thesis committee for immense support.

Thanks to the people I interviewed at the IDP camp in Abuja and to Comdr. Ishaya Phillips Habana (of blessed memory), a commander with the National Drug Law Enforcement Agency in Rivers State, for conducting those interviews with me.

Thanks to the many experts who interviewed with me, especially John Onyeukwu, the deputy chief of USAID programs in the northeastern states of Borno, Yobe, Adamawa and Lake Chad Basin, and Richard Ali, a lawyer engaged in conflict resolution and peacebuilding in the Sahel.

Thanks to the Longleaf Writers Conference for giving me the opportunity to workshop a chapter of *Fine Dreams* as a scholar.

Thanks to friends and colleagues in the Association of Nigerian Authors, Rivers State Chapter, and to Alhaji Denja Abdullahi, the former national chairman.

Thanks to Dennis Masi, D. Marcus Chucxz, Ndubusi Daniel Okeah, Chinomso Ihenagwam, Oguegbu Chinyere Vivian, Abdullahi Maikanti Baru, Emmanuel Azi, and Emmanuel Eke for support.

Special thanks to the Agbonjagwe Foundation and to the management and staff of Lee Engineering and Construction Company, especially Chief Dr. Leemon Ikpea, the chairman.

Finally, special thanks to God, the Holy Trinity. Without him, this novel would not exist.

JUNIPER

JUNIPER PRIZE FOR FICTION

This volume is the twenty-sixth recipient
of the Juniper Prize for Fiction,
established in 2004 by the
University of Massachusetts Press
in collaboration with the
UMass Amherst MFA Program
for Poets and Writers, to be
presented annually for an outstanding
work of literary fiction. Like its sister award,
the Juniper Prize for Poetry established
in 1976, the prize is named in honor
of Robert Francis (1901–1987),
who lived for many years at
Fort Juniper, Amherst, Massachusetts.